APPLE BLOSSOM B&B

A SMALL TOWN, SOUTHERN ROMANCE

SWEET TEA AND A SOUTHERN GENTLEMAN
SERIES
BOOK 3

ANNE-MARIE MEYER

For my reader who fell in love with Bash.
I hope I did his story justice.

PROLOGUE

SWEET TEA & SOUTHERN GENTLEMAN

Bash

This is not your problem.

I stared at the closed door in front of me. I could still see the shocked look on Abigail's face as she stared at me through her puffy eyes and tear-stained cheeks, and it ignited my desire to slay any dragon that dare hurt her. The thought of her in distress caused my heart to pound, so I closed my eyes for a moment, willing myself not to care.

She wasn't my girlfriend. She was Anders'. She wasn't mine to protect. It was Anders' job to protect her. All of the muscles in my body felt like springboards and any slight movement would set them off. But it didn't change the fact that she'd come here looking for her boyfriend...not me.

She'd made that pretty clear. I could still hear the bite to her tone when she said, "It's a job for my *boyfriend*."

My fingers curled into a fist. I wanted to punch Anders for not being here. For not fielding that for me. I wasn't in Harmony to connect. I wasn't here to make friends or be part of a community. I was here to hide away, and Abigail was making it impossible for me to do that.

I didn't need people. I didn't need Anders, and I certainly didn't need Abigail. If she was in trouble, that was her problem. Not mine...

You're an idiot.

I growled as I opened my eyes and headed for my bedroom. In one swift movement, I swept my keys and wallet into my open hand and grabbed my cap and hoodie from the chair next to my open door.

I'd find her sister and nephew, make sure that they were okay, and then I would walk away from Abigail forever.

There was no way Anders was going to help. He told me that he was headed to the pub to drink away the stress of the day. I should have stopped him. I would have had I known that Abigail was going to show up. And now her problems were mine.

I pulled my cap onto my head as I headed out into the parking lot. Once I climbed into the driver's seat, I slammed the door and shoved the key into the ignition. I threw the car into reverse and sped out of my parking spot.

As soon as I got onto the main road, I rolled my shoulders and took in a deep breath, forcing my tense body to relax. It didn't work. I was stressed, and the only thing that could calm me down was finding her sister so I could get Abigail out of my life for good.

I drove to the outskirts of town. The first place I would go if I wanted to disappear was a different town. You go where people don't know who you are.

The sign for Powta came into view, and a few seconds later, I spotted a gas station. I clicked on my blinker and turned into the parking lot. I drove past the pumps and between two very faded white lines. I turned off my engine and climbed out.

The bell on the door jingled as I pushed into the small shop. The smell of day-old hotdogs and soda syrup filled my nose. There were two older men in trucker hats sitting on faded red benches with a table between them. The noise drew their attention over to me. They frowned as their gaze drifted from my shoes to my cap. Not wanting to start anything, I tipped my head forward, making sure that my hat covered my face...really, my scar. I turned away as I shoved my hands into the front pockets of my hoodie and headed to the cash register.

"Good even' to you, darling." A plump woman with greying hair pulled up into a messy bun and a front tooth missing greeted me as I approached. She had on a name tag that said Tabitha. "What can I get for you?"

I glanced out the window toward the gas pumps and then back to Tabitha. Her overly lined eyes narrowed, and I could tell she was sizing me up. So I forced a smile, knowing how my appearance came across.

"I'm looking for my sister," I said.

"Who's your sister?" she asked as she smacked her gum between her teeth.

"She's about, yea high," I said as I stuck out my hand. I knew how tall Abigail was, and I prayed that they were similar.

"Okay." Tabitha continued to stare at me. "You're going to have to give me more to work with."

I nodded. "She has dark hair. Pale skin." At this point, I was just describing Abigail.

Her eyebrows went up.

"She had my nephew with her." I brought my hands out in front of me like I was carrying a baby.

A spark of recognition passed through her eyes. "You men and your lack of attention to detail." She tapped her long fingernails on the counter. "I saw your sister. About thirty minutes ago." She blew out her breath. "She looked a little worse for wear. And that baby? He was non-stop screaming. Right, Earl?" She tipped her face toward one of the men in the back, who just grunted his response.

"That's her," I said, praying that it was, in fact, Abigail's sister and I was not about to head out after some strange woman. I glanced through the front windows. "Did you see which way she went?"

Tabitha waved her hand toward the road. "She headed north."

I nodded as I turned to head toward the door.

"You ain't going to buy anything?" Tabitha's voice stopped me short.

I shook my head and pushed through the door before she could say anything else. The door closed on her muttering breath. I quickened my pace as I headed toward my car and slipped onto the driver's seat. I could see Tabitha glaring at me through the window as I peeled past and took a left onto the road. It was good that I was going in the right direction, but houses were quickly being replaced with trees. And with all of the random side streets, the chances of finding Abigail's sister were becoming slimmer and slimmer.

I slowed as I came to the first street and peered down it.

Nothing.

I continued down until I came to the next one.

Fifteen minutes later, I still hadn't found her.

On a whim—or out of complete frustration—I turned off on the next side street and sped down it. I cursed myself when a dead-end sign loomed in the distance. *Stupid.* I pushed my hands through my hair and prepared to make a U-turn when a figure up ahead caused me to stop.

A woman was sitting on the curb. She was hunched over her knees, and her dark hair hung across her face. I straightened out my car and slowly drove until I was right next to her.

She startled and looked up, and when I saw a baby in her arms, my heart began to pound. I threw the car into park and opened the door. By the time I rounded the hood, the woman was standing. She tilted her body away from me as if she were trying to shield the baby, who was screaming.

"What do you want?" she asked. Her face was dirty, and her cheeks were tearstained. I could feel her pointed gaze as she stared at me through her hair.

"I'm a friend of Abigail's," I said, keeping my voice low. I raised my hands in an effort to show that I wasn't going to hurt her.

Her eyes widened. "Abigail?"

I nodded. "She's dating my roommate, Anders." Those words tasted bitter on my tongue, but I shoved those thoughts from my mind. It was the truth, and I wasn't going to get anywhere by ignoring the facts.

"Anders," she whispered. I could see her body relax.

"Are you okay? Is the baby?" I nodded toward the screaming child.

She shifted, and the baby came into view. His face was so scrunched up that I couldn't see his eyes, and his mouth was open, his face bright red. She bounced him a few times and then glanced over at me with a look of desperation. "I can't get him to stop crying." Tears filled her eyes, and my heart ached for her.

"May I?" I asked as I extended my hands.

She looked skeptical for a moment before she nodded and handed him to me. I brought him to my chest, not really sure what I was doing. I bounced him a few times, and his wail faded to a whimper.

"Why don't you two come with me?" I asked as I

motioned toward my car. Then I glanced up to the sky. Grey clouds were rolling in, and I feared that any minute now they were going to open up and downpour on us.

She glanced over at my car. I could see that she wasn't sure what she wanted to do, but then she closed her eyes for a second before she opened them back up. "Okay."

I smiled, hoping to come across as supportive instead of creepy, as I headed toward the passenger door. I pulled it open and held it as Abigail's sister started to climb in. She paused.

"What's your name?" she asked. Her gaze was tired when it met mine.

"Bash."

She studied me before she nodded. "Sabrina. And this is Samuel," she said as she settled down on the seat and reached out to take the baby.

Once they were both buckled in, I shut the door and jogged around the car. From the way Samuel was crying and how tired Sabrina looked, a trip to Harmony Medical Center seemed to be in order. There was no way I was going to just leave her with the baby alone in their apartment. And I didn't know where Abigail was.

I knew that I couldn't rest until Sabrina and Samuel were safe. Then I could leave. Then I could walk away from Abigail and never look back.

It wasn't until we were just about to pull into the emergency room parking lot that the sky finally opened up. I dropped Sabrina and Samuel off at the front doors and then hurried to find the nearest parking spot. I sprinted through the rain and in through the sliding doors.

Sabrina was hovering near the entrance with Samuel, who had calmed and was quietly staring up at the lights above him.

"I don't—I don't have insurance," Sabrina whispered. Her eyes were wide as she stared up at me. I could see the fear in her gaze, and it made my heart squeeze. I wanted to protect her. She was important to Abigail, which meant, no matter how hard I fought my feelings, Sabrina was important to me.

"Don't worry about it. I'll take care of the bills," I said as I moved my hand to her back and gently led her over to the reception desk.

It didn't take long for them to call her back. I remained seated while Sabrina stood. She took a few steps forward before turning to look at me. "Aren't you coming?" she asked.

I raised my eyebrows and then nodded. "I can come."

Relief flooded her face. She turned, and I kept pace with her as we followed the nurse through large swinging doors and into an empty room. I kept to the corner as the nurse ran the vitals on both Sabrina and Samuel. Then she settled them down on the bed and motioned for me to follow her to the hallway.

I glanced over at Sabrina, but her eyes were closed. Samuel was happily sucking on a bottle the hospital provided. They looked content, so I followed the nurse out of the room.

"Has anyone ever talked to you about postpartum depression?"

I blinked. "What?"

"Your wife. We think she might have postpartum depression."

"My wife?"

The nurse stopped. "Is she not your wife?"

I shook my head. "Um, no. Sorry. She's a friend's sister. We were all out looking for her, and I just happened to find her."

"Oh."

Just then, my phone rang. I pulled it from my pocket and glanced down.

Abigail

"I'm going to need to take this," I said, and she nodded as I turned away.

"Hello?" I asked, bringing the phone to my cheek.

"Bash?" Abigail sounded panicked, and my heart ached for her. I took in a deep breath, knowing that this was probably the last time we were going to talk before I had to leave.

"Abigail?" I said, reveling in the feel of her name on my tongue.

"I need your help. I'm...I'm on highway 80. My car's smoking, and I don't know what's wrong. I haven't been able to find Sabrina, and I'm freaking out. I went to the pub to find Anders, and he was drunk, and now..." Her voice dropped to a whisper. "Now it's raining on me."

I hated that I wanted to save her. I hated that I wanted to be the knight she didn't seem to want. If I could, I would take away all of her pain.

"I'm going to be right back. I have another patient to check on," the nurse said.

I nodded, but before I could respond, Abigail's voice drew my attention back to the phone. "Oh my gosh. You're with someone. I'll just—"

Then the line went quiet.

"Abigail?" I asked. I pulled the phone from my cheek; the call was over.

I stared down at it, trying to figure out what I was going to do. But my fingers had a mind of their own, and before I knew it, I'd pressed the call back button. I waited, but she didn't answer, and it went to voicemail.

Frustration built up inside of me. Why did she care if I was with someone else? She was with Anders.

A few seconds after I hung up, my phone chimed again. I glanced down to see Abigail's text.

Abigail: Hey, don't worry, you sounded like you were busy. I'll just contact a tow truck driver.

I cursed under my breath and shook my head. This woman was being ridiculous.

Me: Where on 80 are you?

Abigail: I think I remember exit 195, but really, it's no big deal. You don't have to come. I'll find someone else.

Like hell she would. I wasn't going to be able to think until I knew that she was safe. And since I wasn't her boyfriend, it would be strange for me to call later to check up on her. I was going to pick her up and bring her back to safety. That was the only way I was going to be able to keep my head on straight.

That seemed like too much to put into a text, so I kept my response simple and texted a quick, "Okay," before I slipped my phone into my pocket.

I checked in on Sabrina, who was fast asleep with a snoozing Samuel next to her. I nodded as I left the room and headed back out toward the lobby.

Luckily, the receptionist wasn't busy, so I left my contact information stating that I would take care of the bills. Then I gave her Abigail's contact information as Sabrina's next of kin. She jotted it all down before peering curiously up at me. I just gave her a quick smile and headed through the sliding doors and out to my car.

The rain was pouring now, but I didn't slow until I pulled up behind Abigail's car. My entire body went into autopilot as I pulled open the driver's door and ducked out into the rain, praying that she was safe. Relief flooded my body when her driver's door opened and she climbed out.

I parted my lips, preparing to explain why I was here instead of her boyfriend. Instead, she threw her arms around me, wrapping them so tight that my entire body froze. My mind swam with questions as fear clouded my thoughts.

And then, my body told my mind to shut up, and I

pushed my fear aside as I wrapped my arms around her and pulled her against me. I took in a deep breath, the sweet smell of her shampoo filling my senses. I closed my eyes as I committed to memory the feel of her body against mine.

I was never going to be the same.

"She's safe," she whispered. Her voice was muffled by my shirt and the rain.

"Sabrina?" I asked. The nurse must have called Abigail.

I felt her head nod against my chest. "And Samuel is safe."

I couldn't see her expression, and I feared that she was upset. But there was no way I was going to loosen my grip on her. "That's good news, right?" I wanted so badly to make her happy.

I heard her sigh and sink further into our hug. The movement and sound sent ripples of pleasure down my back. "It's great news." Her voice was soft and melodic. When she pulled away, my arms ached for her to return.

When her gaze lifted to meet mine, my heart stopped. Tears were streaming down her face, mixing with the rain. I hated seeing them. I hated that she was hurt. "Then why are you crying?" I asked as I reached up and wiped away a tear that was rolling down her cheek.

She didn't flinch or pull away. Instead, she held my gaze. The look in her eyes confused me. All I wanted was to tell her that I cared. That I couldn't stop thinking about her. That I wished she were mine instead of Anders'.

Her lip quivered. "I felt so alone and worried. But now... now she's safe."

I hated myself. I hated that I let her walk away from the apartment earlier. That I'd been a jerk to her. I should have helped her. I should have been there for her. If she only knew how much I wanted to be the man to protect her and take away all of her worries. "I'm sorry you felt alone."

Her gaze met mine once more as a soft smile stretched across her lips, making my heart sing. "I'm not anymore. You're here."

I stared at her, letting her words sink in. And then reality hit me. What was I doing? Why was I holding her like this? Why was I letting myself feel things for her? She was Anders', not mine. And even if she wanted to be, I was in no place to let her into my life.

It was a shit show, and I cared too much to hurt her.

I needed to pull back. I needed to put a chasm of space between me and her. I would take her to see her sister, and then I was going to leave. I would walk away forever even though the very thought crushed my heart.

Abigail was not mine.

And she never would be.

1

BASH

SWEET TEA & SOUTHERN GENTLEMAN

My father's house was dark. The moon shone behind it, and only a lone window in the top left of the mansion was glowing.

I punched the code into the box next to the large iron gate and waited for it to swing open. It took a moment for the code to register, and then slowly the gates parted, letting out a groan that echoed into the dark night sky.

I stared at the driveway reaching out in front of me and took in a deep breath. My fingers tightened against the steering wheel, causing my knuckles to turn white.

"What are you doing?" I asked myself. I closed my eyes and slowly let out the breath that felt as if it were choking me.

Memories of pain. Memories of death flooded me like a river bursting through a broken dam. The dam that I'd used to keep my memories at bay these last five years had been demolished in one phone call.

Emery.

When I saw her number flash on my screen after I dropped Abigail off at the hospital, my entire body went numb. Why was she calling me? We hadn't spoken since the funeral—since she slapped me across the face and swore she would never forgive me. I almost didn't answer, but I wasn't strong enough. If she was calling me, it couldn't be good.

Her words were quick and curt. "Your father is about to pass. He's asking you to come. It's the least you can do."

I don't remember what I said or if I even said anything at all. All I remember doing was nodding. And after a few seconds of silence, she hung up, leaving me sitting on my bed with my phone pressed to my cheek.

I was on the soonest flight to New York, and now I was sitting in the driveway like some idiot who didn't belong but couldn't stay away.

The gate began to close, so I pressed the gas and narrowly missed scratching the back end of the car as it closed behind me. My headlights illuminated the pavement ahead of me, and I started the long climb up the driveway to the front door. I pulled into one of the side spots—the one I used to park in when I would visit—and turned off the engine.

Every part of my body felt numb as I pulled open the door and climbed out. The sound of the door slamming rattled in my brain as I slipped my keys into my pocket and pulled my suitcase from the back seat. My hand strangled the strap as I crossed the driveway to the stairs that led up to my father's multimillion-dollar mansion.

I didn't even have time to knock. The door opened before my fist landed.

"Sebastian." Nicholas' frame filled the doorway, and the light behind him cast shadows across his face. He was older now. His forehead wrinkles deepened as he frowned at me. His white hair was slicked back and thinner.

"Nicholas," I said, my voice deeper with emotion than I liked. I shifted my luggage into the other hand and nodded to him.

His gaze dropped to my hands for a moment. "I'm glad you came."

His words hit my gut like a sucker punch. I didn't deserve to be missed. I didn't deserve to be welcomed back. I deserved to disappear from their lives, so they could find a way to be happy.

Silence coated the distance between us making me acutely aware of how much time had passed and how much had changed. There were unspoken words between us. I could scarcely bring myself to even think them. I dropped my gaze to the porch floor.

Seconds ticked by so slowly that I feared we were moving backwards. He sighed, strangling the silence before he stepped to the side and waved me in. "Your father will be glad to see you."

I scoffed but then covered it up with a cough. Nicholas'

gaze nearly bore a hole in my face, but I didn't look at him. I wanted to get this reunion over with and then go to bed and try to get some sleep. I knew life would be a frenzy tomorrow—the life of a Torres always was—and being well rested was the best way to prep for battle.

We walked in silence as we climbed the massive stairs in the center of the foyer, which led to the second floor. I kept a few feet behind Nicholas as he made his way down the long hallway to my father's door. I remembered standing outside of it many times as a child, waiting for him to come out to play with me. But the door never opened.

Now it sat open, and the soft beeping of medical equipment could be heard from inside. Nicholas walked into my father's room like it was a common occurrence. I was paralyzed as I stood just outside of the doors, not ready to even peer inside of the room.

I closed my eyes as my emotions rose to my throat, choking me.

I wanted to run away. I didn't want to be here, and I knew my father didn't want me here. Emery had called me, yes, but that didn't mean *he* wanted me here. After all, he was the one who had told me I wasn't fit to carry the Torres name and that, from that moment on, he was no longer my father and I wasn't his son.

He hadn't stopped me as I hurriedly packed my bags. And when my car drove away, he hadn't followed after me.

I was officially cut from the family. And I'd accepted

that. After all, if it weren't for me, my younger brother, Carson, would still be alive. His wife would still be happy, and their son would still have his father.

I was the reason my family was torn apart.

I didn't blame them for banishing me. They treated me like I deserved to be treated. I shouldn't have been drinking that night. I should have called a cab. I shouldn't have insisted that Carson come with me. I'd seen the worry in his gaze as he assessed me. And when he said maybe I should sleep the alcohol off, I brushed him off as a sissy and pushed him into my car.

To this day, when I close my eyes, I can still hear the crunch of metal and, in the distance, Carson's faint moan of pain.

My life changed in a matter of seconds, and I swore that I would never come back here. Yet, here I was, facing the past that I'd tried so hard to stay away from.

"Come on." Nicholas appeared in the doorway, snapping me from my thoughts. My gaze met his as he nodded toward my father's bed. "He's asleep."

I swallowed, hating how weak I felt. I took a step forward, acutely aware of the way the marble floor felt under my feet. The vibrations of my movement rattled through my body with each step until I was standing next to my father's bed, staring down at it.

He'd aged in the last five years. His hair was thinning and completely white. His skin was ashen and so pale I could see the blue veins running through it. His eyes were closed, and his hands were placed at his sides. The only thing that hinted of life was the slow, methodical way his chest rose and fell and the soft thrumming of his heartbeat that came from the monitor next to him.

"Does he know I'm here?" I whispered, tilting my head toward Nicholas, who was standing next to me.

From the corner of my eye, I saw Nicholas shake his head. "He's not really aware of much right now. The doctors keep him on heavy pain killers."

Tears clouded my sight. I didn't want Nicholas to see, so I focused my attention back on my father. My hands were clasped in front of me. I felt like a child awaiting reprimand from their parent. Like, any moment, he was going to wake up, and the disappointment that I knew he felt would slap me across the face once more.

Unable to continue staring at my father, I blinked the tears away and turned to Nicholas. "Why did Emery want me here?" I lifted my gaze to meet his.

He reached up and rubbed his shoulder as he sighed. "Timothy is asking about his family. I guess she just wants him to know you guys before things change forever."

"Timothy?"

Nicholas nodded. "Your nephew."

I closed my eyes for a moment. I wasn't sure I could face my nephew. The boy my brother never knew about. Emery hadn't yet known she was pregnant when Carson died. And I left before he was born. I'd seen some tabloid pictures of her holding the baby, but after that, I made a point of never looking at magazines again.

"I'm exhausted," I said as I stepped past Nicholas toward the door. I needed to get out of here before the walls closed in on me and I suffocated under the pressure. I needed a hot shower and liquor. But after the accident, I swore never to touch a drop of the stuff. So I was just going to have to settle for a hot shower and a restless night's sleep.

The sound of Nicholas' shoes on the marble as I made my exit told me that I wasn't alone. He had more to say to me, but I wasn't sure I was ready to hear it.

"Bash," Nicholas said as I quickened my pace.

I didn't want to stop, but it wasn't fair to him. He was like an uncle to me. And even though my father disowned me, I knew Nicholas still cared. He was as loyal to my family as any outsider could be. If anything, I should be grateful that he'd taken care of the mess I'd left in my wake.

"What?" I asked, turning to face him once more.

He studied me for a moment before he glanced at the floor and sighed. "I'm glad you came. I know it wasn't easy for you, but..." His gaze made its way back to me. "Your father misses you. It's good for you two to see each other once more."

I raised an eyebrow as his words settled around me. Then I nodded, my grip on my luggage tightening. "I hope so." Then I turned and made my way down the opposite hallway to my old bedroom.

Once I got inside, I shut the door and took a deep

breath. I glanced around the room, startled that it looked nothing like it had when I left. My father erased every part of me. The posters that dotted the walls and the trophies that lined the shelves had disappeared. The walls were painted a pale grey, and the room felt more like a hotel than my childhood bedroom.

I tossed my luggage onto the nearby armchair and then headed into the bathroom. I flipped on the shower and pulled off my shirt. Just as I turned to face the shower, my scars caught my attention. I turned so I was facing them head-on. The jagged pink lines were a reminder everyday of what I took. Of the life that was no longer here because I'd been an idiot, thinking that I was untouchable.

I should have died that night, not Carson. He would have done more with his life than I could do. He would be a father to his son and build a family with his wife.

And here I was, hiding in town after town, running away from my life.

Steam slowly crept down the mirror, hiding my shame from view. I cursed as I stripped down the rest of the way and climbed into the shower. I leaned my arms against the shower wall and dropped my head, hot water pounding my back.

I knew I shouldn't have come. I knew I should have packed my bags and run so far away that no one knew who I was or what I did.

But the fact that Emery wanted me here gave me hope.

It was stupid, but that flicker of hope was keeping me alive. There might be a chance that she would forgive me. And perhaps then I would start to forgive myself.

But if that hope was snuffed out, I didn't know what I was going to do. Or if I would have a reason to keep living.

2

ABIGAIL

SWEET TEA &
SOUTHERN GENTLEMAN

I blinked as I stared at Sabrina. Her gaze was focused on the screen, and the sound of reporters barking questions filled the silent room.

Bash was the one who found her?

How...When...Why?

So many questions were rushing through my mind, and yet I couldn't focus on a single one.

"You know Sebastian Torres?" Penny asked, stepping forward and giving me something else to look at other than my sister.

Sabrina glanced over at her and nodded. "Yeah. He was the one who found me and Samuel." Sabrina's gaze drifted down to Samuel, who was cooing in Penny's arms. A flash of regret passed over her face, and my heart ached for my sister.

I still hadn't asked her why she'd run away with Samuel

—part of me feared her answer—but she promised me that she was going to go to therapy and take her medication like the doctor prescribed. I had hope for her future, even though it was clouded with a twinge of fear that I would come home to an empty house one day.

"So, Sebastian was here? In Harmony?" Penny glanced between Sabrina and the TV.

It was strange to me that Penny knew him. Or the fact that Bash was the heir to a multibillion-dollar company, and yet, he was Anders' roommate.

I thought I knew the man, but it turned out that was far from the truth.

"What a strange world," Penny breathed out as she shifted Samuel to her other hip and walked over to Dad. He was sitting on the couch with his arm slung over the back and his ankle resting on his knee. He was studying his phone, obviously bored with the conversation.

"He said he knew you." Sabrina was standing next to me now, her gaze trained on my face.

I blinked a few times, bringing myself back to reality, and then nodded. "He's Anders' roommate." My gaze drifted to the TV. "Er...was." Bash was now standing next to a beautifully dressed woman with flowing blonde hair. She was holding the hand of a little boy whose tight ringlets matched his mother's. They were standing awkwardly in front of a large New York skyscraper while reporters took pictures and demanded answers.

"Who's that with him?" I asked no one in particular.

Thankfully, Penny didn't question why I wanted to know. Instead, she handed Samuel off to Dad and made her way over to me. "That's Emery."

"Emery?" I repeated. The squeezing of my heart must have impaired the blood flow to my head because my brain felt like mush. "Is that his son?" The words came out a whisper.

Penny shook her head. "She's the wife of Sebastian's brother. And the boy is his nephew." She sighed. "Carson died not knowing that Emery was pregnant. Poor girl had to do it all on her own." Her gaze drifted to Sabrina as silence fell between us.

"Oh," was all I could say.

Penny walked over to the kitchen and started digging around in a brown paper bag.

"So, what happened to Carson?" I asked, not wanting the conversation to end. I still had so many questions, and I doubted there would be another time I could ask them and it not be strange.

Penny was unwrapping a sandwich. She took a bite before she sighed. "It was a car accident. Sebastian was driving drunk and crashed the car. Carson didn't make it. It broke Alexander's heart and tore the family apart. Especially since the boys lost their mother when they were very young."

"...with Mr. Torres on his death bed..." a reporter's voice broke through our conversation. We both looked over at the screen as they flashed a video of a man lying in bed with monitors all around him.

"And as you can see, there's little hope that the family can be mended in time." Penny's voice was sad, and for a moment, the memory of our relationship with Dad flashed through my mind.

A sadness crept into my chest as I stared at Bash. The weight he must have been carrying had to be immense. No wonder he was so withdrawn and short with me. I knew what a loss like that could do to a person. And to be the reason a loved one was no longer here? That kind of pain had to be immeasurable.

"That's tragic," Sabrina said, drawing my attention over to her. She sat on the couch next to Dad, still tense, but I could tell she was trying. She cooed at Samuel, who giggled and blew her a spit bubble.

Regardless of Bash's history, he'd found Sabrina and brought her home safely. I wished he'd told me that he was the one responsible. Then I could have thanked him before he left. I doubted that I was ever going to see him again, and that...made me sad.

"Your father and I have decided to spend a few weeks here in Harmony," Penny said, obviously finished with the conversation about the Torres family.

I pushed Bash from my mind and turned to face her. "Really?"

Penny nodded. "We want to spend more time with you girls, and the ladies in Magnolia have the newspaper under control. They said I could take as long as I needed." Her gaze drifted over to Sabrina, who had shifted so she was fully on the couch with her head tipped back and her eyes closed. "We want to make sure things are settled here," she whispered.

I nodded, a lump forming in my throat. I was grateful that they were so willing to help out.

Penny must have sensed my mood because her hand enveloped mine as she took a step forward. "I'm so sorry you had to go through this alone. If we'd known how bad it was..." She closed her eyes. "It wasn't fair to ask you to shoulder this all on your own." She opened her eyes, and I could see the tears that had formed there. "Hopefully, we can take on some of that stress."

I swallowed and nodded, not sure if I could respond. All of what she said was true, but I loved my sister. I would walk to the ends of the earth for her.

"It's okay. We understand. We're a family, and we'll figure this out together." Penny patted my hand and smiled up at me. "Why don't you go shower and take the day off? Your dad and I will spend time with Sabrina."

I gave her a weak smile, hoping she could see my gratitude, and then squeezed her hand. She ushered me into my room, where I took a hot shower and dressed. I needed to get to the shop soon if I was going to be there for the morning crowd. I ran a comb through my wet hair and quickly braided it.

When I walked out to the living room, Dad and Sabrina

were asleep on the couch, and Penny was on the rocker, giving Samuel a bottle. She gave me a soft smile as I grabbed my purse and keys and headed out.

I wasn't sure of the logistics of them staying—it wasn't like staying at the Apple Blossom B&B was cheap—but I was grateful for them, nonetheless. It was nice leaving the apartment knowing that Sabrina and Samuel were going to be watched over. My shoulders felt light as I pulled in behind the shop and turned off the engine. I climbed out of my car, and I glanced toward the fence where I'd first met Bash. When he'd been digging in my trunk, looking for the chipmunk who had stowed away.

His dark hair fell over his face, hiding the scar on his cheek. His eyes were dark and mysterious, and in that moment, I just figured him to be a strange man. But now, now I knew why he looked so lost. So broken. And my heart ached for him.

Then I felt ridiculous. He wasn't mine to worry about. He was Anders' friend and the son of a billionaire. He was home, and I hoped he would get the chance to fix what had broken in his past. Second chances were powerful. I was living proof of that.

I sighed as I made my way to the back door and unlocked it. I flipped on the lights as I walked through the store. Once I'd tucked my purse in the back office, I grabbed my apron hanging on the back wall and slipped it over my neck. I surveyed the glass case next to the register and breathed a sigh of relief. Fanny must have stayed late baking and refreshing stock.

It looked like the only things I needed to do today were make lemon poppyseed muffins and brew the coffee. That, I could do. I needed the mindless work to keep my anxiety about Sabrina and my thoughts about Bash at bay.

Work was the perfect antidote.

I was an hour from opening, and in the midst of scooping muffin mix into the tin, when I heard a rapid soft knock at the front of the store. I glanced up to see Shelby peering back at me. Her cheeks were flushed, and her eyes looked wild. She was either evading a serial killer or incredibly excited.

I raised my finger to let her know that I saw her, rinsed my hands, and headed toward the door. Shelby didn't even wait for me to fully open the door. She skittered by me and let out a squeal.

Mystery solved. She was incredibly excited.

"I'm so glad you're here," she said, her voice breathless as if she'd been running all over town.

"Where else would I be?" I asked as I locked the door and turned. I was excited for my friend, but her energy was a lot after the last 48 hours I'd had.

She was so euphoric that she didn't even notice my sarcasm, which I was grateful for. The last thing I wanted was to bring my friend down. She deserved all the happiness in the world, and I had a suspicion as to what she was about to tell me.

"You and Miles?" I asked as I gave her a sly smile and headed back to the kitchen.

Her jaw dropped open. "Am I that transparent?"

I shrugged. "I've only known you for a few weeks, but Miles has been the only person to have this kind of effect on you. Good or bad."

She giggled as she sat on the barstool. Then slowly, she slid her left hand into view. A three-stone diamond ring sat on her fourth finger. My jaw dropped as I glanced up at her. I figured that they'd made up. Getting engaged was not on my bingo card.

Excitement bubbled up as I rushed around the counter and pulled her into a hug. "Engaged?" I exhaled as I pulled back.

The look in Shelby's eyes was euphoric as she nodded. "He proposed this morning."

I dropped my jaw. "And you're here? Why? Shouldn't you be celebrating?"

She wrapped her left hand with her right and then brought them to her chest. "Well, we want to get married...tomorrow."

I sputtered. "Excuse me, what?"

Shelby shrugged. "We've known each other pretty much all of our lives. We're done waiting. I want to be his. Forever." She must have sensed my skepticism because she added, "And it's just at the courthouse. We're planning a big celebration later this year." She sighed before a contented look came across her face. "I just want to be his wife, and I don't want to wait."

I studied her before I smiled. "If that's what you want."

She nodded. "I want you to be my maid of honor."

I raised my eyebrows before emotions flooded my chest. "I'm honored." Then I hesitated. I didn't want her to ask out of obligation. "Are you sure?"

"Of course. You're one of my best friends. And you were there when I needed you." Her gaze met mine. "Please?"

I gave her another hug. "Of course. I'd love to."

She giggled, and I made my way around the counter to focus on the muffins. I enjoyed her company as she told me their plans for a simple wedding. They were going to go to the courthouse and get married there. Then they'd treat their wedding party to a meal at the diner.

I loved the simplicity and how happy it made Shelby. And for a brief moment, I wondered if I could find the same happiness. The conversation shifted to Sabrina and the events from the night before. I slipped the muffins into the oven and started in on the story—keeping Bash out of most of it.

I really didn't want to rehash what had happened with him. My thoughts were already so muddled that talking about it would just make me more confused.

Shelby must have finally sensed my mood. A look of worry flooded her eyes. She raked her gaze over me as she furrowed her brow.

"You still worried about Sabrina?" she asked.

Once again, my emotions rose to the surface, coating my throat and making it hard to swallow. But I forced those feelings back down and nodded. "Yeah. Even though she's safe, I can't shake the fear I felt when I walked into that empty apartment." I blew out my breath. "It's nice, though. My dad and Penny are here for some time, so I'm going to rely on them." I gave her a weak smile.

She shook her head. "I'm so sorry. I should have been there. You should have called me."

"You had your own thing going on."

She pursed her lips. "Still. I could have helped."

"Well, in the future, I'll call you. But I'm hoping I won't have to."

She eyed me, but that seemed to appease her. She drummed her hands on the counter before she stood. "I should get going. I've got a few more things to do around town before I head back to the inn." She stopped halfway to the door. "I'll text you details about tomorrow, 'kay?"

I nodded.

She grinned and then hurried through the door, the bell jingling on her way out. I was so close to opening, that I didn't lock the door after her. The smell of coffee brewing and muffins baking wafted through the air, causing me to relax. Even with the confusion of my life lately, I could always depend on this shop and my ability to make delectable morsels.

I was a failure at love, but my baked goods made you feel like you were wearing a warm blanket on a cool fall evening.

The bell jingled, and I glanced over, half expecting to see Shelby coming back with one more wedding detail to tell me. My jaw dropped when I saw Anders standing there with damp hair, his hands shoved into his front pockets and a sheepish look on his face.

"Anders," I said.

He winced as if I'd slapped him across the face. I could tell he felt bad—which he should. "Abigail." He pushed his hand through his hair. "Can we talk?"

3

CLAIRE

SWEET TEA &
SOUTHERN GENTLEMAN

My 1999 Ford Focus rattled as I pulled up the long gravel driveway leading to the Apple Blossom B&B. I exhaled as the large three-story house came into view. My mother's pride and joy. The only child of hers that she actually cared about.

The only child she actually loved.

I never thought I'd come back here. At least, not as a single, mid-twenties woman with no romantic prospects and no *real* job to speak of. But apparently, I was a glutton for punishment, because here I sat, staring at my impending doom.

I navigated my car to the back of the house, where the workers parked, and turned off the engine. The sun was shining down on the yellow-painted siding, which contrasted beautifully against the bright blue sky. For any guest, Apple Blossom B&B was a picturesque mansion in small-town North Carolina. A stone's throw from the beach.

But for me, it was a place that reminded me I was a disappointment and would never amount to anything.

It was my mother's house. My overbearing, control-freak mother, who would never be happy with me as her daughter.

I lingered in my car for a few minutes, gathering the courage to head inside. My stomach had been in knots ever since my older sister, Cassie, texted me that the siblings decided I was to be sent to Harmony Island to help our mother recover from a broken hip. I'd delayed my departure for as long as I could—she didn't need my help while she was at the hospital.

But after a panicked call from Rose, the hostess at the B&B and the woman who'd practically raised me, I packed up my car and made the eleven-hour drive straight through. I was exhausted and ready for a nap. And yet, I couldn't bring myself to leave my car even though the place in front of me contained thirteen beds.

I yelped when three rapid taps on my window pulled me from my thoughts. My hand flew to my chest to calm my pounding heart as I leaned forward to roll the window down. My nerves began to calm as I stared into the familiar grey-blue eyes of Rose. She was older now. Her grey hair was pulled up into a bun, and her smile lines had deepened.

Her cheeks were pink, and she looked both flustered and excited to see me. "Claire, why on God's green Earth are you sitting in that car like a nobody. Get out here and give me a hug." Her hand was on the door handle, and before I could speak, she'd pulled it open.

I had to hurry and unbuckle before she tried to yank me —still attached—from the car. I stumbled a bit on the gravel as my feet hit the ground, but Rose was there to wrap her arms around me and pull me close. She smelled like her namesake, and the familiarity of her embrace brought feelings of nostalgia that I hadn't thought I could feel anymore.

She was the mother figure that my own mother never was. She'd protected me. Snuck me out after curfew so I could watch a movie at Harmony Park with my friends. She even defended...

I swallowed against the lump in my throat as thoughts of Jax came rushing back to me. It felt ridiculous that I still thought about him from time to time. After all, I was certain he'd moved on from this small town—even though I'd never brought myself to ask my mother to confirm. It felt futile to think about him when I was sure he never thought about me.

Why would he?

After all, I was the one who walked away. I was the one who broke his heart. If anything, he would hold a séance in my name and curse me from now into the afterlife.

So allowing myself to think about him was ridiculous. I didn't have the right to be sad or to miss him.

"How's mother?" I asked as I pushed the thoughts of a man I once loved from my mind. Rose had finally relinquished her hold on me, and I was going to seize the moment of freedom to grab my luggage.

Rose sighed. "She's doing better. The doctor thinks she can come home in the next few days. He did say we need to build a ramp, but you know your mother, she's refusing to. Her and her historical house nonsense." Rose stood behind me, and as soon as I pulled my luggage from the car, her hand found the handle and pulled it away from me.

"I've got it," I said, but Rose just tut-tutted me.

"This is how I stay young. If I just sat back and let people take care of me, I'd be six feet under right now." She drew the cross over her chest and then ended with a kiss to her fingertips before she looked up to the heavens. "I promise the good Lord every morning that I'll keep working hard if he keeps me around."

I chuckled as I followed her across the gravel and up the back steps. I forced Rose to let me hold the door open for her, despite her mumblings about me being a guest.

The kitchen smelled like chicken and dumplings, which made my mouth water. I peeked into the bubbling pot as I walked past, and the smell made me pause and inhale.

"You always did love my chicken and dumplings," Rose said as she glanced over at me.

I closed my eyes. "I still can't find a recipe as good as yours."

"And you never will. There's a secret that I put into each pot I make. And that secret...will go to the grave with me."

"Is it love?" I asked as I followed her toward the back of

the house. Toward the bedroom I'd shared with Cassie until she moved out.

"Well, yes, that. But it's not the only thing," Rose said, giving me a mysterious smile as she turned the handle and pushed open the bedroom door.

"I'll get it out of you one day," I said as I stepped into my old room. Not much had changed here. My old posters and trophies dotted the room along with Cassie's even older memorabilia. Even though my mother wasn't motherly, she had a hard time getting rid of things, which is why our room had remained untouched all of these years.

"I tried to dust in here this morning, but as you can see, it floated up into the air and just came back down. I was hoping maybe...you could dejunk this room?"

I scoffed and feigned a hurt expression before I broke out into a smile. "I'll see what I can do." I moved to plop down on my bed. I half expected a puff of dust to shoot up around me, but the bedding looked freshly washed. No doubt because of Rose. "But I don't plan on being here that long."

"Oh, hush your face," Rose said as she wiggled her forefinger at me. "Now that I have you back, you're never leaving."

I smiled at her. If coming back only meant spending time with Rose, I wouldn't ever want to leave. But being back in Harmony meant being back in the presence of my mother, and no amount of chicken and dumplings or Rose's rib-crushing hugs could make up for that.

Rose's cheeks flushed as her smile faded. "I know you and your mom have struggled. I'm not denying that. But she's glad you're here. I know she was disappointed that the others didn't come."

Guilt coated my stomach. Did she know that I was only here because I'd been assigned to? Did she think I came voluntarily? Would she think worse of me if she knew the last place on earth I wanted to be was here, helping my mother?

"Have you seen her?" I asked, deciding to avoid the topic altogether. It was easier than dealing with what her words meant.

She moved to lean against the doorframe and nodded. "I was there bringing her some toiletries this morning." She grimaced. "She's definitely giving the nurses a run for their money. Demanding that they let her go. That this isn't the time for her to be stuck in a hospital."

I frowned and glanced around. "Trouble at the B&B?" My mother may not have formed emotional attachments to her children, but she would never do anything to jeopardize her precious B&B.

Rose shook her head. "This place will stand the test of time." Her gaze drifted to the window. "But something is happening in Harmony. You can feel change in the breeze."

"Harmony Island? Changing?" I scoffed. "I didn't think this place even understood the word."

Rose glanced back at me. "You'll feel it as you wander around town. There's a buzz in the air."

"Huh." I smoothed the comforter next to me. "Does Mom know what's going on?"

Rose shrugged. "You know your mom. She's always had her ear to the ground—"

"—and her nose in everyone else's business." The words were out before I could stop them. They sounded more bitter than I'd intended. The tone wasn't lost on Rose as her gaze met mine.

"Sorry," I whispered. I knew Rose loved my family, and that included my mother. She just didn't have the history with her that I did.

"I don't pretend to know what it's like growing up with Missy Willis as your mother. But I do know that when it came to Jax—"

"Don't." I raised my hand. I didn't want to think about him much less talk about him. "Please, don't talk about him."

"But I thought you might want to know—"

"Rose!" I groaned as I grabbed a nearby pillow, flopped back onto the bed, and covered my face with it. "Don't!" I cried into the fluff.

I paused, waiting to see what she was going to do. When I felt it was safe, I slowly lowered the pillow. The room was silent, so I brought it down to my chest and hugged it. "Let's make a pact that Jax is an oh-no-no word. And we don't say oh-no-no words."

Rose quirked an eyebrow. I could see the desire to tell me what she wanted to say twinkling in her eyes, but she just nodded. "Jax equals an oh-no-no."

I clapped my hands together before I pointed in her direction. "You've got it!"

She studied me before she shook her head. "You're insane."

"But you love me."

She narrowed her eyes. "I guess."

I flipped to my stomach and picked at the top layer of the comforter. "So, what is the plan for the rest of the night?"

Rose pushed off the doorframe. "I'm waiting for the last guest to arrive, then we are packing up the chicken and dumplings and heading to the hospital."

"Um, *we*?"

She nodded. "Rest up, 'cause we are leaving in an hour," she called over her shoulder as she headed into the hallway.

"Um, *we*?" I called again after her retreating frame, but she didn't turn around.

I groaned as I flopped back once more and covered my face with the pillow. There was no way I had the energy to deal with my mother tonight. I was surviving off just a few hours of sleep.

I needed a full night's rest for seven consecutive days if I had any chance of surviving for even a minute in my mother's presence. I hugged the pillow to my chest as I curled up onto my side and closed my eyes.

The problem was, Rose was just as stubborn as I was. If she wanted me to go...I was going.

Whether I liked it or not, I was going to come face-to-face with my mother tonight.

Yay me.

I GOT EXACTLY thirty minutes of sleep before Rose came in and jostled me awake. I didn't want to get up. But she threatened to withhold food, and from the way my stomach was growling, there was no way I was going to let that happen. So, I rolled off the bed.

The car ride to Harmony Medical Center was quiet. Rose hummed along with some Neil Diamond, and I held the steaming hot container of chicken and dumplings in my lap so it wouldn't spill.

My gaze was focused outside as Rose drove. I was shocked at how much had changed. So many homes now lined the shoreline that it was almost impossible to see the ocean as we drove into town. I glanced over at Rose, and she nodded.

"I told you. Change is in the air."

"Literally," I breathed as we passed by a chain-link fence that had fabric covering it as if they didn't want any passersby to see what was happening on the other side.

As we drove into downtown Harmony, things began to look more normal. A sense of nostalgia washed over me as we passed the little mom-and-pop shops that I grew up visiting. The streets were lined with people walking out of the shops or entering. I didn't recognize anyone, but that was normal for a tourist town.

At the far end of town was Harmony Medical Center. Rose pulled into the parking lot and turned off the car. I opened the door and juggled the container of soup as I stepped out. With it safe in my hands, I used my foot to shut the door behind me. Rose was waiting for me to join her, and when I did, we walked side by side through the doors and into the lobby.

The medical center was quiet. There were two receptionists at the front talking to each other in hushed voices. An older man who I didn't recognize was lounging in one of the chairs with his legs extended in front of him and his hands resting on his chest as he watched the TV on the wall.

Thankfully, Rose knew where to go because she marched right up to the receptionists, who quickly ended their conversation and turned to face her with a smile.

"Good evening, Ms. Monteque. Here to see Mrs. Willis again?" the blonde receptionist asked as she swiveled her chair so she was facing her computer.

Rose nodded. "This time I'm here with her youngest daughter, Claire."

Both sets of eyes shifted over to me. They gave me a smile, and all I could do was nod.

"She's been moved to room 7."

The sound of the automatic doors unlocking drew my attention as they slowly swung open. I waited for Rose to lead the way, and I followed behind her. Just as we cleared the doors, she stopped.

"Heaven forbid," she said as she tapped the bottom of her palm to her forehead. "I left the things your mother wanted me to bring in the car." She started to back up, and as I parted my lips to protest, she waved her hand toward the rooms lining the hallway. "You'll be fine. Room seven is just down the hall and to the right."

She turned on her heel, and before I could think of what to say, she was out of earshot of the protests racing through my mind.

I stood there, holding a huge container of soup, debating on whether or not I should proceed without Rose. It seemed ridiculous. After all, she was my mother. I should be able to visit her without Rose as a buffer. But I never felt comfortable in the presence of my mother. It was sad, but that was the truth.

I took a deep breath, but as I scanned the waiting room, I saw that the two receptionists were curiously watching me. I knew they weren't judging me, but embarrassment coursed through my body, nonetheless. Knowing I couldn't stand out here, waiting for Rose, I nodded in their direction and took off through the doors before they shut on me and I had to ask the receptionists to open them again.

The doors slowly creaked closed behind me. The locking sound of the mechanism echoed in the quiet hallway. I took another deep breath and then started toward the room. I couldn't quite remember the number, but Rose had given me some general directions, so I tried my best to follow them.

I settled on the fourth door on the right. I stood outside for a moment, then pushed down on the handle. The beeping sound of monitors could be heard behind the drawn curtain.

I closed my eyes for a brief moment before I said, "Hey."

It wasn't eloquent or Shakespearian, but it was the only thing that came to mind. Mom didn't respond. There was a rustling sound before the curtain was yanked open.

It took a moment for my brain to catch up with what I was seeing. Instead of staring into the bright blue eyes of my mother, a familiar cool blue stared back at me. He was older now, his jaw covered in a five-o'clock shadow. His blond hair was mussed, and his clothes were wrinkled. He looked as confused as I felt as he stared back at me.

"Claire?" he asked, his familiar deep voice sent shivers across my entire body.

"Jax?"

4

BASH

SWEET TEA & SOUTHERN GENTLEMAN

This was why I left.

I blinked as the spots from the flashing cameras blinded me. My cheeks hurt from smiling, and my tie was too tight. Emery was standing next to me with Timothy at her side. I hadn't had time to process anything that was going on. All I knew was my father wanted Emery and me to make an appearance at Torres Towers so that the rumors about the family losing control of the business could be put to rest.

But all of it felt fake. I was fighting the urge to sprint from the paparazzi and hide out in a hotel until I could process the feelings raging inside of me.

Emery hadn't seemed phased when she saw me. And that had me on edge. I half expected her to slap me across the face as I held the limo door open for her, but she barely acknowledged me. Instead, she stepped out, waited for

Timothy, and then gracefully crossed the courtyard without so much as a glance in my direction.

Her indifference was worse than her rage. When she'd hated me, at least it had fueled the hate I felt for myself. But not acknowledging me left me feeling hollow and empty. I couldn't imagine that she'd forgiven me, so this reaction had to be for the cameras. Once we were alone, she was going to let her true feelings show.

"Come now," Nicholas said as he stepped in front of the cameras with his arm extended. "You have the pictures you need. These two are needed upstairs." He nodded toward the front doors, and I followed behind Emery and Timothy as they made their way inside.

It was quieter in the lobby. My dress shoes and Emery's heels made tapping sounds on the marble floor as we made our way to the elevators. The anxiety in my gut made me feel like I was suffocating. I pulled at my collar in an effort to relieve the tension as we waited for the doors to open so we could board. At least when we were outside, I could keep my distance from Emery. But I was about to step into an elevator with the physical proof of my past. I wasn't sure I would emerge in one piece.

"I'll take the stairs," I mumbled under my breath as I made my way to the door along the far wall.

"But it's on the twentieth flo—" Nicholas called after me, but his words were cut off as the door swung shut behind me.

I didn't care if it was on the hundredth floor. I needed

space and a way to burn off all the energy currently coursing through my veins.

I was puffing when I finally got to the top floor and yanked the door open. My suit coat and tie were draped over my arm, and my top buttons were undone. Nicholas was waiting in the lobby for me with his arms folded across his chest. He quirked an eyebrow.

"Feel better?" he asked as I walked up to him.

I just growled my response, but he didn't back down. He motioned toward the bathroom right next to the elevator. "Get presentable. We're in conference room A."

I glanced in the direction he motioned before I nodded and headed into the bathroom. I emerged with my tie on and my suit coat still draped over my arm. The receptionist at the front desk glanced over at me before she quickly dropped her gaze back to her computer.

I nodded but didn't speak as I passed her. I was fairly certain that I was the gossip for the day. The boss' son reappears after five years. It had to be the scandal of the year. I hated that I was once again the topic of conversation. This was not what I wanted.

I wanted to hide. Forever.

I found conference room A in a matter of seconds. The door was closed, but from the side window, I could see the backs of Emery and Timothy's heads. They were sitting across from three men in suits, who I could only assume were my father's lawyers. No doubt primed to talk about the future of the company.

A company that I did not want to be a part of.

That was Carson's dream. Taking over our father's business. Shifting it into new ventures and new countries. He would go on and on about it at family dinners, much to my father's delight.

The fact that the seat next to Emery was empty only made his loss that much more poignant.

Nicholas must have seen me standing outside the door. A moment later, it opened, and he was standing there. His gaze met mine, but if he saw the panic in my gaze, he didn't acknowledge it. Instead, he waved me inside and instructed me to sit next to Emery.

I hesitated, but the entire room seemed to be waiting for me to sit down, so I pulled out the rolling chair and sat down with my back straight. I could feel Emery tense next to me when my arm brushed hers. I pulled away as quickly as I could to put some space between us.

Her reaction gave me hope. She still hadn't forgiven me...good.

She should never forgive me.

"Good morning," said the man sitting in the middle. He had a handlebar mustache and was dressed in a Gucci suit. It was a strange contrast, but if he worked for my father, he was trustworthy. "We're here to discuss the future of Torres Investments as your father nears..." He paused. "As your father's condition worsens."

Emery and I both nodded in unison. I instantly stopped moving my head and vowed to remain still for the rest of my time here. This was really for Emery, not me. And I'd be damned if I took this away from her.

"We'll start with Sebastian."

All eyes turned to me. Well, all eyes except Emery's. She just remained rigid next to me. Which I appreciated. I feared what I might do if I had her attention.

"Okay," I managed out.

"Torres Investments owes Deveraux Construction Management a substantial amount of money due to a bad deal last year."

I hesitated. I thought I'd read something in the business section of the newspaper about that, but as soon as I saw my father's name, I crumpled it up and threw it away.

"Your father and Richard Deveraux came up with a solution that seems advantageous for all involved." He paused and glanced at the men on either side of him. Almost as if he were verifying what he was about to say. "Torres Investments will merge with Deveraux Construction, thereby erasing all of the debt, under one condition." The lawyer glanced up at me, meeting my gaze head-on. "You marry the daughter of Richard Deveraux, Emmeline Deveraux."

I stared at him, his words reverberating in my ears. But my brain could not process what he was saying. "I'm sorry, what?" I asked.

He sighed. "It's strange, but it's the arrangement your father was able to put together. It's not unheard of. Using marriage to solidify company deals."

"Marriage." I tapped the table with my forefinger. "To a strange woman I've never met." I met the lawyer's gaze.

"You can say no. But if you do, Torres Investments will have to liquidate a significant amount of the company to pay off the debts."

"Then do that."

"Well, it's not that simple. It is more beneficial for both parties to keep Torres Investments intact than to sell off portions for a fraction of what they're worth." He cleared his throat as he glanced over at Emery. "Plus, a portion of the company that we will have to dissolve is included in Mrs. Torres' inheritance. The portion your brother was working on..."

An icy chill fell over the conference room. As the anticipation of his next word hung in the air. As if he realized whose presence he was in, he just cleared his throat and stared down at the papers in front of him.

"Then he should do it." Emery's voice was quiet, but her words were direct.

The sudden sound of it startled me, and I glanced over at her. "What?" I asked before I could stop myself.

Emery was staring straight ahead. "Marry Emmeline. Finally do something good for this family." She closed her eyes and a tear slipped down her cheek.

Her words felt like daggers in my chest as I stared at her. She was still hurting because of me. She hadn't forgiven me. She still hated me as much as I hated myself.

Slowly, she turned to face me. Her expression was cold,

but I could see the rage boiling behind her gaze. She studied me for a moment before she brought her gaze back over to the lawyer.

In that moment, I knew what I needed to do. If marrying some strange woman would protect Emery and Timothy, then I would do it. It wasn't like I had anyone in my life I was giving up. I would do anything to put a bandage on the gushing wound I'd created five years ago.

"Okay," I whispered.

"Okay?" the lawyer asked.

I nodded. "Okay. I'll marry Emmeline."

5

ABIGAIL

SWEET TEA & SOUTHERN GENTLEMAN

I didn't know what I wanted to do. Anders was standing in front of me with his hands clasped in front of him and a contrite look on his face. I'd ask him to meet me for lunch, not bombard me at work. I had half a mind to tell him to hit the road. But Sabrina was home safe, and even though things had gotten out of hand at the pub, Anders had been drunk. It wasn't new to me. Dad had also struggled with his liquor, and he was still in my life.

I didn't mind sober Anders.

But I couldn't stand here talking with the shop so close to opening, so I moved over to the faucet and turned it on. "Talk," I said as I dunked the dirty mixing bowl into the sudsy water.

From the corner of my eye, I watched as Anders hesitated and then made his way up to the counter. He glanced around, and I could feel nervous energy emanating off of him. That made me feel guilty. He'd made one bad decision. Was I going to hate him forever because of it?

When he glanced over at me, I offered him a soft smile. His eyebrows went up, and I could see his shoulders relax.

"Coffee?" I asked just as the oven beeped. "A fresh muffin?"

His signature half smile made my heart sing as he dropped down onto the nearest barstool. "Both sound amazing."

I finished washing the bowl, rinsed it, and set it on the drying rack. Then I grabbed a nearby dishtowel to dry my hands. After pulling the muffins from the oven, I used a pair of tongs to snatch one out. With a steaming mug full of coffee in one hand and the muffin on a plate in the other, I headed back over to Anders.

He took them, his fingers brushing mine briefly. I felt his gaze on my face, but I didn't react. Instead, I just pulled my hands back and returned to the sink.

"How's your sister?" he asked after a few bites of the muffin.

My stomach knotted at the question. Last night was a time I never wanted to relive. "She's home now. My dad's down from Rhode Island with his wife. They're keeping an eye on her."

He nodded. "That's good. I'm glad she's safe."

Tears pricked my eyes as the memory of almost losing her rushed back to me. I focused on the dough paddle I was washing and forced myself to get a grip.

Suddenly, Anders appeared next to me. He reached out and turned off the water. "Hey," he said as he took the paddle from me and set it in the sink. "Hey," he repeated as he took hold of my shoulders and turned me to face him.

A tear slipped down my cheek. I wasn't quite ready to forgive him, but I was tired. I was emotionally spent. I knew I should tell him that he disappointed me last night, but I didn't have the energy. And he looked like he felt bad.

A sob escaped my lips as I leaned in and dropped my forehead onto his shoulder. I closed my eyes, and he wrapped his arms around me, pulling me close. He held me as I cried into his soft cotton shirt. I hadn't realized until now how much I'd been holding inside.

My cheek was wet, which brought me back to reality. I pulled back and winced when I saw the giant tear stain on his shirt. "I'm so sorry," I whispered as I reached out and rubbed the mark.

He glanced down and shook his head. "It's fine. It'll dry." Then he dipped down, forcing me to meet his gaze. "I'm just worried about you."

I held his gaze before I took in a deep breath and blew it out. I took a step back in an effort to ground myself in the present. "I'll be okay," I said.

The look on his face told me he didn't believe me.

"I will eventually be okay," I said, this time with a forced smile.

He crossed his arms and shifted so that he was leaning against the counter. His gaze never left my face, so I reached out and grabbed a napkin to dab under my eyes. I was certain I looked a mess, but his soft smile eased the pain that had settled in my chest since I discovered Sabrina missing.

"You don't always have to be the strong one," he said as he reached out and tucked my hair behind my ear.

I snorted. "Yes, I do." Ever since Mom died and Dad left, I had to be the strong one for Sabrina. And with her sudden disappearance, I was beginning to realize that I was going to have to be the strong one forever.

He studied me. "Well, maybe it's time that someone helped you shoulder that load."

His gaze intensified as he stared at me. I understood his meaning, but I wanted to clarify. I didn't have the energy to get into any kind of relationship where we played games. I'd already let myself have feelings for Bash, which had been futile. He had a past I had no idea existed, and there was no way I could take on that kind of uncertainty.

If Anders was willing to be there for me. To help me with what I needed. Then I was willing to consider another chance for us. But I needed it to be as uncomplicated as possible.

"About last night..." I paused as I watched for his reaction.

He looked uncomfortable as he shifted his weight so that he was fully standing. He dropped his gaze for a moment before he pushed his hands through his hair. "I'm so sorry that I let you down."

I chewed my lip. The truth was, I didn't have the right to

come down on him. After all, we hadn't been dating that long. He had the right to go to a pub and get as drunk as he wanted. But I didn't like the way he'd treated me in the pub, and that was something we needed to discuss.

"Believe me, if I'd known you needed me that night, I wouldn't have let Benson convince me to do shots with him." His gaze was on me now. His crystal-clear eyes were a marked difference from the murky ones that had greeted me last night. He looked like the Anders I remembered. The one I'd gone looking for that night.

"I don't remember a lot, but Jax informed me that I had my hands on your hips and was trying to..." His voice faded as he closed his eyes.

I swallowed, remembering how I felt when he wouldn't let me go.

"I understand if you don't trust me. But I promise, I would never hurt you. I was drunk, and I know that isn't an excuse, but let me make it up to you." He opened his eyes and dipped down to catch my gaze. "Please?"

I released my bottom lip from between my teeth. It felt raw, and I didn't need a bleeding lip for the rest of the day. "You hurt me," I whispered.

He nodded. "I know."

I wasn't perfect. My life was a testament to that. I depended on people giving me second chances, so I would do the same with Anders. "Okay. We can try again," I said, offering a soft smile.

His grin spread across his face. He leaned in and

wrapped his arms around my waist. I giggled as he hoisted me into the air. I wrapped my arms around his neck as he spun me around. The feeling of lightness had me throwing my head back, laughing. I was done with that night. I was ready to let go of everything that had happened and just move on.

The only thing still clouded in a shroud of confusion was Bash...but he was gone now. And I doubted that I would ever see him again.

6

CLAIRE

SWEET TEA &
SOUTHERN GENTLEMAN

"Wha—what are you doing here?" Jax glanced around as if the walls of the hospital room held the answer to his question.

"What are *you* doing here?"

His gaze was back on mine as he stared at me. "What are *you* doing *here*?"

This conversation was going nowhere. "I'm here to see my mother." I stepped to the left and gestured toward the bed but then froze.

Sitting where I expected my mother to be was Jax's grandfather. He was scooping pudding from the cup in his hand. He must have sensed my gaze because he paused and looked up at me.

"Claire Willis?" he asked as he stared at me through his tiny circle glasses.

Embarrassment hit me like a ton of bricks. My entire

face warmed as I dropped my gaze and spun to the door. Then I raced from the room, ready to run back to Rose's car, demand she drive me home, and never come back.

But the hallway was currently occupied by an elderly lady being escorted on either side by a nurse, making my getaway impossible. Not wanting anyone else to be a witness to my embarrassment, I spotted a supply closet, yanked open the door, and hurried inside.

Just as I moved to shut the door, a hand grabbed the edge and pulled it open. I yelped and jumped back, worried it was a hospital worker about to chide me for going where I shouldn't. But to my horror, Jax filled the doorframe as he looked quizzically at me.

The silence that engulfed the space between my body and his was deafening. We just stood there, staring at each other. Neither of us said a word. It seemed like reality dawned on him faster than it did on me. He glanced to the side and blew out his breath.

"When did you get here?" he asked, his gaze slowly making its way back to mine.

I hugged the container of soup to my chest like it was my lifeline. It was a miracle that I hadn't dropped it during my hasty retreat.

"A few hours ago," I managed out, which surprised me. I had the strength to speak. That was unexpected.

He studied me. "Why were you in my grandfather's room?"

"I didn't know that was your grandfather's room."

"Really?"

I nodded. "I was looking for my mother. She just had hip surgery, so I was coming with Rose to visit her and bring her some soup." I held out the container as proof.

His gaze drifted down to it and paused. "Is that Rose's famous chicken and dumplings?" The corner of his lips tipped up into his signature half grin.

My heart pounded, and I hated that, after all of these years, I reacted this way. "Yes."

He licked his lips. "I haven't had that in a long time."

I just stared at him as the memory of us eating around the kitchen table with Rose while my mother was at a weekend retreat flashed through my mind. Back then, we had to sneak around because my mother didn't approve of our relationship. I hated that the only thing he missed was Rose's cooking. But there was no way I was going to ask him if he remembered those times as well.

He sighed, ran his hand through his hair and down to his neck, and leaned his head back like he was stretching his muscles out.

I hated that my gaze drifted to his forearm and then down to his bicep that was now straining against the sleeve of his t-shirt. Why hadn't he gotten ugly? Why was he now an older, more attractive version of the boy I fell in love with?

It wasn't fair.

He glanced down at me before I could pull my gaze

away and flashed a knowing smile. My cheeks heated, but I did my best to force down that reaction and remain calm.

"Is your grandfather okay?" I asked, deciding to turn this conversation away from me and toward him.

"I'm sorry?" He leaned forward as if my question had caught him off guard.

"Your grandfather." I nodded at the door. "He's here. So, is he okay?"

Jax shoved his hands into his front pockets. "He was just getting a stent checked out. He had a heart attack earlier this year and was having some pain." His expression became strained.

My heart lurched for him. I knew how much he loved and depended on his grandfather. I scoffed, and my reaction seemed to throw him off guard. His gaze whipped to mine as he frowned.

My eyes widened. "I'm so sorry. That wasn't for your grandfather. I'm just..." I took a deep breath. "I just figured you'd left Harmony. I never imagined that you would still be here, eight years later."

In an instant his expression turned stoney. His entire body stiffened, and he took a step back. It was as if my words had reminded him of something, and he was doing all he physically could to walk away from it.

"I have to get back," he murmured as he turned and grabbed the door handle. He didn't wait for me to respond. Instead, he barreled out into the hall, barely missing Rose, who was staring into the closet with wide eyes and a confused expression.

He was gone before Rose could speak, so she zeroed in on me.

"What was that about?" she asked as she walked into the closet to join me. Her gaze drifted from wall to wall before she turned back to me. "Why were you hiding out in a closet with Jax?"

I didn't want to talk about it. But Rose looked like she wasn't going to let me leave until I spilled the story.

"Why didn't you tell me he might be here?" I asked. That was good. Change the focus to her.

She quirked an eyebrow. "Excuse me?"

I nodded, feeling good about this. "You've been here. How did you not know that his grandfather was staying down the hall from my mother, which means that there was a chance we might run into him?"

Rose shifted her weight and folded her arms across her chest. Her expression was daring me to keep going. And I did.

"I mean, you know how I feel about him. How I left things. A little warning might have been nice. Instead, I barrel into the room, and Jax is standing there, staring at me. His grandfather is in bed eating pudding, and he's staring at me. I look like this—" I make a circle motion in front of my face. "The least you could have done was give me a heads up. Instead, I'm standing there like an idiot as he stares me down. I try to run out of the room, but he follows me, and now..." I let out my breath. My whole body ached, and exhaustion had finally settled in. "I'm standing in a supply closet, holding a container of soup, and looking like an idiot."

The last few words left my lips as a whisper. Tears pricked my eyes. I was already emotional about having to see my mother. I hadn't thought I'd need to protect myself against seeing Jax.

This trip was already off to a terrible start, and it was only day one.

Rose's stance softened as she dropped her arms, crossed the room, and stood in front of me. She took the container of soup from my arms and set it on the shelf next to us. Then she wrapped her arms around me and pulled me in close.

"There, there," she whispered as she ran her hand down my hair like she did when I was little.

I didn't want to, but I leaned into her and closed my eyes, letting the tears slip down my cheeks. I let out the breath I didn't know I'd been holding and let the familiarity of Rose's embrace release the tension in my body. The truth was, I wasn't ready to face my past. Nothing could have prepared me for what I had just gone through.

There were two people I'd been running from, and I'd just gone into battle with one and come out alive. In a few minutes, I was going to face the other demon from my past. If anything, I should be grateful to get both over with so quickly. Then, I could disappear into one of the rooms at the B&B and never come out.

"Seeing Jax was inevitable," Rose said, as she pulled

back and tucked my hair behind my ear. "It was good for you to get that meeting over with."

My gaze met hers. "So, you did know he was here?"

She shook her head. "I really didn't. And I would have warned you if I did." Her smile turned soft as she took the container of soup from the shelf. "But I'm happy that you got your first sighting over with. It's time you two made amends so you can move on." She raised an eyebrow, and I knew in an instant what she was thinking.

"I'm not single because of Jax," I said, as I wiped at my tear-stained cheeks and took in a deep breath. Then I fluffed my hair, hating that my mother was going to see me post mental breakdown. She was going to have words. I could already hear them.

"Right," Rose said, giving me a wink before she yanked open the door.

I followed after her, ready to defend myself. "I'm not. Have you seen the men available to date?" I asked, probably a bit too loud. A couple standing near the wall turned to stare at me.

Heat burned my cheeks as I fell in step with Rose and lowered my voice. "The pool of men has gotten sadder and sadder." I winced and shook my head as the profile pictures my friend Lydia had sent me rushed through my mind. "No, thank you."

"I don't believe you," Rose whispered as she turned down the hallway and stopped in front of a closed door.

"About the men on dating apps?" I scoffed. "Well, you should. It's pathetic."

"No, not that." Rose shook her head. "That Jax isn't the reason you're single."

This woman knew me too well. The truth was, when I was a little tipsy on wine and had been listening to a few too many Mariah Carey songs, I might have pulled out his phone number from my old journal and typed it into my phone. But I'd never called him. So, it really didn't count.

But there was no way I was going to admit that to Rose. Not when she was so close to my mother and there was the slightest chance it could get back to Jax. My mother didn't like him before, and I was certain nothing had changed to make her like him now.

Not that my love life needed my mom's approval, but I wasn't going to play with that fire again. I broke his heart once, and it would be cruel to open that door again. Jax needed to move on, and so did I.

We were two pieces of a puzzle that were never meant to fit together. Even if in the past we'd felt like we were meant to be together, we weren't. And I needed to be okay with that.

"Mom's room?" I asked as I nodded toward the closed door. I was ready to get away from the conversation even if facing my mother was the only way to do that.

"Yes," Rose said.

"Great." Not wanting to run into Jax in the hallway again, I turned the door handle and pushed into the room.

The curtain was closed, and I waited for Rose to enter and walk around it before I went further. I wasn't going to have another Jax situation, so I let Rose go ahead. When her smile widened, I knew who was on the other side of the curtain.

I steeled my nerves for the hurricane I was about to walk into and then moved to stand next to Rose.

Mom's eyes widened when they landed on me. She was sitting up on the bed. She was wearing a pink nightgown that accented her tanned skin. Her white hair was pulled up into a bun at the top of her head. "Claire," she said.

"Hello, mother," I said as I grasped my hands in front of me. I wasn't sure what I was supposed to do. Did I hug her? Shake her hand? Salute her like she was my general? The questions were flooding my mind, rendering me paralyzed.

"We brought you some chicken and dumplings," Rose said as she rounded my mother's bed and pulled the tray toward her.

Mom held my gaze for a moment before she turned to Rose. "That smells amazing."

"It's known to have healing powers," Rose joked as she pulled off the top and then turned toward her purse. "I have the items you asked for," she said as she plopped the bag that she'd gone back to the car for into my mother's lap.

Mom just nodded and set it next to her on the nightstand. "Thank you for that." Then her gaze drifted over to me. "How was the drive?"

I shrugged. I hadn't moved from my spot. I wasn't sure

where she wanted me, and the last thing I wanted to do was get in the way. Missy Willis was particular, and I'd been on the receiving end of her particularity enough in my life. I wasn't going to court more.

"You don't know?" Mom asked, her tone turning curt.

"It was long," I said.

"You know what? I forgot some bowls and spoons," Rose said as she clapped her hands. "I'll go grab some from the kitchen." She patted me on the shoulder as she hurried past.

I wanted to follow her. The last thing I needed was to be left alone with my mother. But if Rose sensed my panic, it didn't stop her. She was gone before I could say anything. It would be strange for me to leave now. Especially since grabbing spoons and bowls didn't require a second person.

I left my gaze lingering on the door for a few seconds before I turned back to my mom. She was eyeing me, her gaze drifting down my body as she assessed me. I could see the words she wanted to say dancing around in her gaze. I sucked in my breath, bracing myself for what was about to come.

"You're skinny."

I glanced down at my body. There was some truth to her words. I often found myself so wrapped up with the animals at the shelter that I would forget to eat. But I wasn't unhealthy. "Okay," I said, not sure what she wanted me to say.

"Don't you eat?"

"Of course, I eat."

She clicked her tongue. "Well, you don't eat enough."

I just stared at her. Were we really going to do this? "I'll eat more," I said with a shrug. I wasn't her baby anymore, and I hated that even as an adult, she still treated me like a child.

She sighed and turned her attention to the window. The sun had sunk beyond the trees, painting the sky in varying shades of orange. "This came at the worst time," she whispered.

Suddenly, I felt sorry for my mother. She looked so sad and broken, sitting in the hospital bed. I took a step closer to her, hoping she'd see it as a peace offering. "It's never a good time to break a hip," I said as I softened my tone.

Her sharp gaze returned to me, and I had half a mind to leave. She wasn't trying to be vulnerable. She was angry, and I was about to face her wrath. "Don't you understand what's going on here?" Then she scoffed. "Of course, you don't. None of my kids know. You four were all too happy to run away from here the moment you could."

I pulled back. When she got like this, I lost the ability to form words and defend myself. I was once again a little girl getting a tongue-lashing because I broke a piece of her precious china.

"We all got jobs out of state. You can't really blame us for—"

"Don't lie to me, Claire Marie Willis. All of you children are ungrateful and unwilling to help me."

"Unwilling? Mom, I'm here. *To help.*" I emphasized the

last two words. She couldn't lump me in with my siblings. Even though they'd basically made me come, Mom didn't know that. I was here, and that had to be worth something.

"You can't help," she said, turning her gaze back to the window.

"Why don't you try me?" I was already here. I might as well be useful. And with Mom in the hospital for the next few days, I could actually do what she asked without her micromanaging me. She might actually see that I was more capable than she believed. "What's going on?"

She was silent for what felt like an eternity before she turned to face me. "They're coming for this town." Her voice dropped an octave. "They are coming for the Apple Blossom, and we can't let them."

7

ABIGAIL

SWEET TEA &
SOUTHERN GENTLEMAN

I felt like a terrible maid of honor. With less than twenty-four hours until the wedding, I couldn't throw Shelby a bridal shower or a bachelorette party. Thankfully, she assured me that she didn't want any of those things. Picking out a wedding dress was all she cared about.

So, the next morning I drove her around town, hoping to find something fast. Thankfully, we found what she needed at the first store, Mattie's Antiques. There, she found a form-fitting white dress that looked like it was from the 1950s. It came complete with a hat with attached netting that looked like a veil.

It was outdated, but Shelby looked beautiful in it.

We then made our way to the salon. While we sat in the chairs to get our hair done, she asked me about Sabrina and Anders. I wondered if she'd seen Bash in the news, but if she did, she didn't ask me about it—which I was thankful for. I was trying my hardest to forget that man, and talking about him would negate all of my hard work.

We left the salon with our hair curled and pinned back at the nape of our necks. Shelby insisted that I invite Anders to the wedding, so I sent off a text as soon as we climbed into my car. I took her back to my apartment—she wasn't supposed to see Miles before the wedding—so we could get dressed and eat a snack before we met up with everyone at the courthouse.

Penny and Sabrina gushed over Shelby's dress—Dad had volunteered to run the shop—and when I came out in the powder-blue satin dress that I'd had stashed away for a special occasion, they oohed and aahed over me as well. We finished up the charcuterie board that Penny had put together, and just as we piled into my car, I got a text from Anders that he would be there.

I drove Shelby to the courthouse. She was nervously bouncing her knee the entire trip there. I glanced over at her, worried about my friend.

"You okay?" I asked. When she glanced over at me, I nodded toward her knee.

She reached out and pressed her hand against her thigh. "Yes."

"You can always postpone," I offered. I knew she loved Miles, but I wanted her to know that he would understand if she needed more time.

She shook her head. "I don't want to wait. I'm just…"

When she didn't continue, I leaned forward. "You're just?"

She sighed. "What if I'm not a good stepmom to Belle?"

I pulled back, shocked that she would say that. "Why wouldn't you be a good stepmom?"

Her gaze dropped to her clutched hands in her lap. "My mom. She wasn't a great mother, and she was a terrible stepmom to Miles." She glanced over at me, her eyes full of tears. "What if that runs in the family?"

If I hadn't been driving, I would have reached over and pulled her into a hug. "That wasn't your fault. You're not your mom."

"So, you don't think it's genetic?"

I shook my head. "Of course not. You love Belle. You're going to be an amazing mom to her."

Shelby's gaze drifted out the window, and I could see her shoulders relaxing. I was worried about my friend, but I knew as soon as I got her to the courthouse and she saw Miles, all of her fears would dissolve into a distant memory. Not wanting to make her feel like she needed to talk, I leaned forward and scanned through the radio until classical music filled the car.

There was a small gathering of people outside of the courthouse when I pulled up. I could make out Miles, who was grinning from ear to ear. He was holding Belle, who was squirming to get down. She had on a pale-yellow dress, and her hair was pulled up into a bun.

Tamara was wearing a red dress and was standing a few

feet away talking to Mrs. Porter. I could feel Shelby's energy as I pulled into a parking spot. Miles must have spotted us because he handed Belle off to Tamara and took off toward us. He was at Shelby's door before she could even get it open.

"You look..." his voice drifted off as his gaze ran over her body.

Her cheeks flushed as she took his extended hand. He helped her out of the car, and I couldn't help but smile at the way he took a step back so he could see her more fully. Then he pulled her to his chest and wrapped his arms around her. She giggled, but it was muffled by his suit coat.

"I was a bit worried you weren't going to come," he said as he pulled back.

Shelby's smile faltered as she reached up to cradle his cheek with her hand. "I told you I'm done running. I'm yours."

He stared at her before bending down and capturing her lips with his. Not wanting to stare, I turned and headed toward the courthouse steps, where the rest of the party was waiting. Just as I landed on the bottom step, a figure appeared next to me. Startled, I turned to see Anders. He slipped his hand into mine as we walked up the steps together.

He was dressed in a dark blue suit and a crisp white button-up shirt that accented his tanned skin. His gaze was forward, but I could tell he knew I was studying him because he was grinning. He squeezed my hand as we approached Mrs. Porter and Tamara, who were swinging Belle between them.

I nodded to Tamara when she waved at me. "I'm glad you came," I whispered to Anders.

"I'm glad you asked," he replied. He extended his hand to introduce himself to Mrs. Porter.

The ceremony in the judge's chambers was short. I choked up when a tear slipped down Miles' cheek as he said his vows. The judge pronounced them husband and wife, and we all whooped and hollered when Miles took that moment to dip Shelby back before kissing her breathless.

Mrs. Porter and I signed the marriage certificate as witnesses before we all left the courthouse and made plans to eat a late lunch at Harmony Diner.

Anders slipped his hand into mine as we walked toward the parking lot. His hand was warm and calloused, and I enjoyed that I felt feminine and protected with it wrapped around my own. A soft smile emerged as I kept my gaze toward the ground.

"That was fun," Anders said, nudging my shoulder with his.

I glanced back at Miles and Shelby. Miles was holding Belle with one arm and Shelby's hand with the other. Shelby looked happier than I'd ever seen her, and it made my heart swell.

I just wished that someday I would find that same kind of happiness.

The parking lot was empty when we parked our cars

outside of the diner. Anders found my hand once more and squeezed it as we walked up to the front door. There was no one standing at the hostess desk, and there was a sign that said, "Seat yourself." Since Shelby and Miles weren't here yet, Anders and I lingered by the entrance so they could pick where they wanted everyone to sit.

The only sound in the place was the normal clatter from the kitchen and the occasional soft cough of a man with a trucker hat, sitting in the far corner reading the paper.

A small boy with curly blond hair sprinted out from the swinging kitchen door. He had a cookie clutched in one hand and was protecting it with his other.

The door swung back open, and Willow appeared. Her hair was pulled up into a messy bun, and her eyes were wild as she searched the dining room. "Jasper!" she yelled when she spotted him in the far corner, shoving the cookie into his mouth as fast as he could.

She almost didn't see us, but as soon as she passed by, her whole body stopped. Her gaze drifted over to us, and I could see her embarrassment through the redness of her cheeks.

"Oh my gosh," she whispered as she smoothed down her apron and turned to face us. "I'm so sorry. I didn't know anyone was in here." She moved behind the hostess stand and bent down before reappearing with some menus tucked against her chest. "How long have you been waiting?" she asked, glancing between me and Anders.

"Just a few minutes. It's okay. We're waiting on Shelby and Miles."

She nodded. "Abigail, right?"

I smiled at her with the hope that it might help her relax. "Right. I own The Shop Around the Corner."

"You saved me a few days back. Or, I should say, you saved Jasper." Her gaze drifted to Anders, and a small crease formed between her eyebrows as if she were trying to figure out if he was the man she'd seen me talking to outside my shop that day.

Desperate not to bring up Bash, I slipped my arm around Anders' elbow and stepped closer to him, hoping she would just move on. She blinked before turning back to me.

"Shelby and Miles?" she asked.

"Miles owns the Harmony Island Inn. They just got married."

Her eyes widened. "Wow. Today? I didn't know."

I shrugged. "They wanted it small, and it was kind of last minute."

The sound of the front door opening drew our attention over. Miles was holding Belle in one arm as he held the door open for the others to enter. They were laughing and talking, and their voices filled the entire diner.

"You beat us," Shelby said as she stepped up to me and wrapped her arm around mine, giving me a tight squeeze. She pulled back, and I could see that she was in heaven.

For a moment, I felt jealous of her happiness. But I

quickly pushed that feeling aside and gave her a big grin. "We're just faster, I guess."

Willow motioned for us to follow and brought us over to the largest table in the back, which seated ten people. After handing out the menus, she took our drink orders and told us she would be back to get our food orders.

We sat and listened to Shelby and Miles talk about their plans for the inn. I'd only seen Miles a few times around town before Shelby got here, and I'd never seen him so happy. He had his arm draped over the back of Shelby's chair, and every time she spoke, his gaze was focused on her.

She was his world, and everyone around them could see that. It made my stomach ache with desire for what they had. I glanced over at Anders, who was watching Shelby talk. His lips were tipped up into a soft smile, and he was nodding along and laughing with everyone else at the table.

Could it be him? Was all this the universe's way of telling me that Anders was the guy for me? After all, Bash was in New York taking over his father's business. He wasn't here. He had a whole other life that I hadn't known about. I wondered if Anders even knew about it.

Anders needed to work some kinks out, but now that he'd seen how sad he'd made me, he was ready to change. Men could change...right?

Not wanting to dwell on my thoughts for too long, I leaned forward and tuned back into the conversation. I slipped my hand onto Anders' thigh, and I felt his body stiffen for a moment before he relaxed and his hand engulfed mine. Shelby finished the story she was telling and met my gaze.

My heart soared at the grin she gave me. My friend was finally happy, and I was thrilled for her. She deserved it.

"Tabitha!" a high-pitched voice drew all of our attention to Betty Lou Thompson who was standing behind Mrs. Porter's chair. Her hair was windblown, and her cheeks were flushed like she'd been on a brisk walk. "I'm so glad I've stumbled upon so many Harmony Island shop owners in one place."

"What can we do for you, Ms. Thompson?" Miles asked as he turned to face her.

"We're hosting a town hall meeting. If Patrick Jorgenson thinks he can sell this town to some construction company, he's got another thing coming." Ms. Thompson straightened her glasses on her nose as her gaze turned razor focused. "He may be mayor, but we're the ones who put him there. He'll have to deal with all of us before we let him take what we worked so hard to create."

She took her time to meet each of our gazes. "Do I have your word that you won't sell and that you'll come tonight so we can strategize what we can do? Seven o'clock tonight at the community center."

I glanced over at Miles and Shelby. They were studying each other as if to ask what the other thought. Not wanting this to distract from their moment—after all, they just got married—I decided to step in.

I turned my focus on Ms. Thompson and put on my

widest smile. "We'll try to make it," I said. When I could see the protest building in her gaze, I shook my head. "I mean, we'll definitely make it."

She pinched her lips together and studied me as if she were doubting my words, but I just kept my smile as big as I could. Just then, Willow appeared with our food and set it down in front of us. With the attention diverted from Ms. Thompson, she must have realized that there was no getting it back, so she huffed and made her way out of the diner, calling over her shoulder that she expected all of us to be there.

The table fell into a soft murmur of conversations as we dug into our food. Anders was quiet, so I nudged him with my shoulder. When he glanced over, I gave him a smile, which he returned.

"Everything okay?" I asked.

He took a bite of his hamburger and nodded. "Yeah." His expression turned thoughtful. "I guess I just don't want you guys to get your hopes up."

I frowned. "Hopes up?"

He nodded as he picked up a french fry and twisted it around in front of him. Then he dipped it into the ketchup before shoving the whole thing into his mouth. He dusted salt off his fingertips. "The construction company that she was talking about? Deveraux Construction? I think the deal has already been sealed. And from what I've experienced with working for them, they are ruthless. They won't let you guys stay." He glanced over at me. "They will get their way."

"Deveraux Construction?"

He nodded.

I dropped my gaze to the chicken sandwich on my plate. I pushed a few fries around before I glanced back up at him. "Well, if they are going to fight, so are we." I gave Anders a grin. "They've never messed with a town like Harmony Island."

8

BASH

SWEET TEA & SOUTHERN GENTLEMAN

The candlelight in the center of the table mixed with the soft orchestra music coming from the other side of the room and made my head pound. My tie felt as if it were choking me, and my shirt, although it was made from the finest Egyptian cotton, felt like sandpaper against my skin. I was out of place.

Nicholas had ordered me an entire wardrobe when I got back from the meeting with the lawyers and insisted that I wear one of the Italian suits he'd picked out for me. It felt strange, having someone so invested in how I looked again. When I was on my own, I did what I wanted, went where I wanted, wore what I wanted. When I'd lived here before, my life had been micromanaged, and I wasn't sure I was ready to have that happen again.

Yet, here I sat, waiting to meet my betrothed.

It was so weird that I was being forced to marry. It

wasn't the eighteen hundreds anymore. Why had my father decided the best way to make a business deal was to force his son to get married?

It was probably to torture me. His last way to force his will on my life. With his dying breath, he decided to yank the future from me that Carson was never going to get. That's what this was about.

I pulled at my collar, the desire to yank the tie from my neck and undo the top button rushed through me, but I pushed that desire down. This was my life now. Fancy dinners. Unbearable music. Lighting that made me squint to read anything. Pretentious relationships that only went skin-deep because everyone was afraid and jealous of everyone else.

My stomach churned at the thought of being here, and a part of me—a part that I'd forced into the lockbox at the back of my mind—longed for Harmony Island. I missed the salty air. I missed the freedom that a small town gave. And I missed...

"Sebastian?"

Images of Abigail's dark hair instantly snapped from my mind, and I turned my attention to who I could only assume was Emmeline Deveraux. Her red hair fell in soft curls around her face, and her bright green eyes stared expectantly at me. She had her hand extended. I pushed my chair back and stood.

"Emmeline?" I asked, taking her hand and feeling extremely awkward as I did it.

"Sebastian," she repeated, this time in a knowing way.

"Bash," I said as I leaned in.

"Bash." The way my name rolled off her tongue and the way she stared at me caused my shirt to itch once more.

"Please." I dropped my hand, rounded the table, and pulled out her chair.

She tucked her hair behind her ear as she made her way over. I pushed her chair in as she sat. Not sure what to do, I just let my brain take over and reached for her napkin to shake it out. She started as I set it in her lap. "Um, thank you," she said, looking quizzically up at me.

I nodded and moved back to my seat. Once I was settled, I reached forward and took a large sip of my water. The waiter had poured it earlier, but I hadn't touched it. Now it felt like an oasis to my parched throat.

"Did I make you wait long?" Emmeline asked as she picked up the drink menu and motioned for the waiter to come over. After ordering some fruity concoction, she settled her focus on me.

I cleared my throat. "Not long, no." That wasn't true. According to my watch, she'd made me wait exactly twenty-six minutes. But I wasn't going to tell her that.

She leaned forward and gave me a large, white-toothed grin. "Good." Then she opened the menu and began to peruse. "Have you decided what you are going to order?"

"Yes."

She lifted her gaze up, and I could see her eyes peering

over at me from above her menu. "You did? What did you decide on?"

"Filet mignon with a side of buttered corn and mash." It was a meal I'd enjoyed as a child. And even though I hadn't had it since I'd left, I figured it was best to stay with what I knew.

"That sounds delicious," she said just as the waiter came to deliver her drink. She folded the menu and handed it to him. He took it and she ordered for the both of us. The waiter nodded along and then promised he would put the order in right away.

Silence filled the space between us once he left. I nervously pushed the utensils around, not sure where to look or what to say.

"This is a bit strange, isn't it?" Emmeline whispered.

When I glanced up, I saw that she'd leaned forward, and her gaze was soft—like she understood what I was going through. She looked kind. Trusting.

I blew out my breath as I leaned back in my chair. "It definitely wasn't what I was expecting when I came home."

She laughed. It was melodious and soft. She lifted the rim of her glass to her lips and took a sip. "I called my dad a bastard and stormed out of the house when he told me."

I snorted. "Wow."

She nodded. "You don't say that to Richard Deveraux. It took a lot of groveling to get back into his good graces."

"Things are good now?"

"I'm here, aren't I?"

I nodded. "But do you want to be?"

She dabbed her lips with her napkin before replacing it on her lap. "We're part of the rich society." She sighed. "Do we ever get to be where we want to be? Besides, it's a necessary evil so I can do what I want."

I quirked an eyebrow. "And what do you want to do?"

She pinched her lips as she stared at the watermark her drink had left on the table. She ran her fingers across the edge of the circle before peeking up at me. "I think we'll have to see how this dinner goes, and maybe..." She narrowed her eyes. "Maybe I'll share it with you."

"Oh," was the only stupid and incompetent thing I could think of to say.

The waiter brought us dinner rolls, and we spent the next twenty minutes snacking and swapping horror stories of growing up as New York elites. The tales were eerily similar even down to the evil headmistresses at the private schools our parents had paid way too much for.

When our food was delivered, we ate in silence, and I was surprised to find I didn't feel like I was going to crawl out of my skin. Emmeline helped me feel at ease, which I appreciated. If I was going to share my life with this woman, it was a bonus that I at least felt comfortable in her presence —and from the way she smiled back at me, I got the feeling she felt the same.

When our plates were whisked away, our waiter asked if he could interest us in dessert. I started to open my mouth—

for some strange reason, I didn't want this evening to end—but I stopped when Emmeline spoke first.

"No, thank you. We're leaving."

The waiter nodded and left the table. I glanced over at Emmeline, wondering if I'd said something wrong. The last thing I wanted to do was return to my father's quiet house and sit in my room while I tried with all my might not to think of the dark-haired woman hundreds of miles away from me, sitting in her bookstore surrounded by the smell of baked goods and coffee.

Being with Emmeline helped me forget Abigail for a moment, and I needed that. I needed to forget that life and focus on my new reality. The one where I could make up for my past mistakes.

When Emmeline glanced over at me, her eyes were shining like she had something devious planned. I felt even more confused. If she was happy, why was she so desperate to call the night off?

"I have some cookie dough at my apartment that's begging to be cooked." She glanced around. "It'll be better than some bite-size dessert that they offer here." She gathered her purse and moved to stand.

I hurried out of my chair and rounded the table before she could reach for her suitcoat, which she'd hung on the back of her chair. I held it out, and she smiled up at me before she slipped her arms in and shrugged it onto her shoulders. We walked, side by side, out to the valet. The man nodded when he saw me and hurried off to retrieve the car that Nicholas had insisted I take.

"Mind if I catch a ride?" Emmeline asked, peeking up at me. "I was dropped off by a friend."

I studied her and nodded. "Sure."

The car was in front of us within a matter of seconds. I reached forward and opened the passenger door, and she gracefully climbed in. Once her legs were out of the way, I shut the door, grabbed the key from the valet, and climbed inside.

It took about twenty minutes to get to her apartment building. She leaned over me to punch in the code to the garage. I pulled back as far as I could go in my seat. Her hair brushed my hand, and the smell of her perfume filled my senses. When she was finished, she pulled back but paused to meet my gaze. I wasn't sure what she was trying to do or what she wanted me to do, so I just sat there, frozen.

I watched as her gaze slowly made its way to the left side of my face.

The scar.

My first instinct was to throw her off my lap. I didn't want her looking at it. I didn't want her asking me about it. With the tabloids, I was certain she knew about Carson. That didn't mean I wanted to talk about it.

Thankfully, she didn't ask about it as she settled into her seat. The garage door was open, so I pulled in and followed her instructions to an empty parking spot. By the time I'd turned off the engine, she had her seatbelt unbuckled and was opening the car door to get out.

I lingered, wondering what I was doing. Why was I going into this woman's apartment? Guilt clouded my mind as I wondered what Abigail would think of me. Would she be disappointed?

Would she care?

Then I shook my head, pulled the keys from the ignition, and climbed out of the car. I was being an idiot. Abigail wasn't mine—she was Anders'. And she didn't care about me. I doubted she'd even thought twice about me.

I was basically engaged to Emmeline. I'd agreed to marry her. I needed to get Abigail from my mind once and for all. It wasn't fair to Emmeline. She didn't deserve a man who was thinking about another woman.

Emmeline was waiting for me as I slammed the car door. She smiled at me as I approached her, and we walked side by side toward the elevators. The ride up to her penthouse was quiet. We stared at the numbers as the car climbed.

"You're going to have to forgive me. I didn't know I'd be bringing someone back with me, so the place is a bit of a mess." She glanced over at me with a sheepish expression.

I shrugged. "I'm sure it's fine."

The elevator stopped, and the doors slid open, revealing her living room. I almost laughed when I saw a few throw pillows out of place and a blanket bunched up on the ottoman. If this was what a mess was to her, she'd faint if she saw the motels and apartments I'd stayed in during my time away.

She hurried around the apartment, picking up a few stray items. Then she motioned for me to follow her to the kitchen.

I stood next to the raised bar and watched her kick off her heels and slip out of her suit coat. The desire to get comfortable raced through me, so I shrugged off my suit coat as well before I loosened my tie and unbuttoned the top button of my shirt. Then I removed the cufflinks that Nicholas insisted I wear and rolled my sleeves to the middle of my forearms.

When I glanced up, I saw Emmeline watching me with an unreadable expression. Her gaze was focused on my hands before it slowly made its way up to my face. When she realized that I was watching her, she dropped her gaze and turned toward the fridge.

"You're not what I expected," she said as she pulled open the door.

Her response intrigued me. "I'm not?"

She spun around with a tube of cookie dough in her hands. Her gaze met mine as she shook her head. "Nope."

I raised an eyebrow. "What did you expect?"

Her gaze drifted down my body before she shrugged, set down the cookie dough, and opened a long, skinny cupboard to pull out a cookie sheet. "I don't know. Just...not you."

I wasn't sure what to say to that. I watched her as she peeled the wrapper off the cookie dough and began to slice it into rounds, arranging them on the sheet. She didn't invite me to join or ask me to help, so I kept to the outskirts of the room, not sure what to do with myself.

She got to the end of the roll, left a small section on the cutting board, and moved to place the sheet in the oven. With the timer going, she grabbed the remaining cookie dough and turned to face me. She broke the chunk in half and handed me the larger portion.

I took it. I wasn't a fan of raw cookie dough, but she was being nice, so I decided to oblige her. She was standing in front of me now, studying me. She broke off a piece of cookie dough and slipped it between her lips as she narrowed her eyes. Then she turned and nodded for me to follow.

"I wanna show you something," she said as she started to walk away. She didn't look over her shoulder to see if I was following her. Instead, she moved with the confidence that I *would* follow...and I did.

She led me down the hallway and into a small room that I could only assume was her office. There was a desk in front of some bookshelves. A small loveseat on the other wall was draped with a crumpled throw blanket, and a pair of heels were tipped over in front of it. I lingered in the doorway while she moved around the room before turning to face me.

"Come here," she said as she sat down on the office chair and shook her mouse to wake up the computer. The lock screen emerged from the dark monitor, and my gaze lingered on it.

It was a picture of Emmeline with her cheek pressed to a man's. She was squinting her eyes and grinning at the camera as she took the selfie. The man was doing the same.

Emmeline quickly typed in her password, and the picture vanished. I glanced over at her, wondering who the man was and what had happened, but I knew it wasn't my place to ask, so I decided to pretend that I hadn't noticed.

"Wanna know my secret project?" she asked as she kept her gaze focused on the screen while clicking on different folders.

"Okay," I said as I moved to stand behind her chair.

She double-clicked on a JPEG, and a picture filled the screen. I stared at it, confused by what I was looking at. The town looked familiar, but...different.

"What is that?" I asked.

She turned to me and smiled. This was the happiest I'd seen her. She twisted her chair a bit to each side as if she couldn't contain her glee. "That is Harmony Island. Deveraux Construction is going to create something magical there."

9

CLAIRE

SWEET TEA & SOUTHERN GENTLEMAN

In all the years I'd lived in Harmony, I'd never gone to a single community meeting. I'd gleaned from overhearing my mom complain about them that they were filled with yelling about property lines and ugly front doors. In a small town, everyone had petty grievances, and the best place to air those grievances was during a public forum.

So, it was a miracle that I was sitting on one of the hard, metal chairs in the middle of the community center's gymnasium. Under normal circumstances, I would have avoided this place like the plague.

"They have lemon cookies," Rose whispered as she slipped onto the seat next to me. She had a yellow-tinted cookie clutched in a napkin in one hand and a cup of steaming coffee in the other.

I glanced over to the refreshment table, which some of the shop owners were gathered around. I felt hungry, but not hungry enough to chance meeting someone I grew up with. I wanted to keep my distance while I was here. No need to dredge up the past.

I folded my arms across my chest and slipped lower into my seat. I didn't want to be here, but I wanted to prove to my mother that I could be an asset to her. It was ridiculous, I knew, but I needed to prove myself.

Betty Lou Thompson was standing in the front, next to a small folding table. She was shuffling some papers around and talking to Betty Godwin. They looked intense as they spoke. If my mother had been here, she would have been in the middle of that conversation with the same amount of vigor coming from her lips.

This town was definitely worked up, and these women weren't going to stop until they had slayed the dragon. From the intense look in their eyes, they were going to pulverize whatever company was threatening their town.

The bells from the clock in the hallway rang out seven times, which snapped both Ms. Thompson and Mrs. Godwin to attention. Betty sat down on one of the seats behind the table as Betty Lou moved to stand in front with her papers now secured to a clipboard that she pressed to her hip.

"Thanks for coming tonight," she said as she focused her attention on the loiterers around the snack table. They must have felt the heat from her stare as they quickly picked up their snacks and hurried to their seats. With the room finally settled, Betty Lou continued.

"It is terrible what Mayor Jorgenson has planned. I was informed that three more businesses were approached by Deveraux Construction with a bid to purchase their place." There was a collective gasp around the room.

I turned to see who it was but then froze. Just behind me and three seats down, I spotted Jax. I almost audibly groaned at how good he looked. He was wearing his ball cap backwards, a pair of jeans, and a fitted hoodie. His jaw was scruffy, but this time, in an intentional way. He had his attention on a woman who was talking a few seats over, so I let my gaze linger.

I wondered for a moment if he was married or dating anyone. I glanced down to his left hand, and his fourth finger was bare...so he wasn't married. But that didn't mean he was single.

Why couldn't men wear something that signaled to everyone that they were taken? It would make my life so much easier.

My gaze drifted up to his face once more, and when I met his stormy blue eyes, I sucked in my breath and dropped my gaze to my lap. What was I doing? Why was I staring? Had he seen me?

My cheeks were on fire. I knew the answer to that question.

Yes, he caught you staring because you're an idiot.

I quickly turned my attention back to Betty Lou. She was introducing a petition she wanted all of the business owners to sign. She handed the clipboard to the person closest to her.

From the corner of my eye, I saw Jax look over at me once...twice...three times. My heart pounded harder each time.

Why did he keep looking at me? Oh, no. Was there something on my face?

My entire body felt like it had been lit on fire as the questions raced through my mind. I lifted my hand up as casually as I could and rubbed the cheek that was nearest Jax. I didn't feel anything. Maybe it was a stain? Had I used a pen recently?

"Why are you so squirmy?" Rose hissed under her breath. Her shoulder brushed mine as she leaned in.

My mind was swimming now. I felt as if the world around me was spinning, and I couldn't catch my breath. This had been a mistake. I knew I shouldn't have come here.

"I need some fresh air," I mumbled under my breath as I hurried to stand. Rose didn't have enough time to shift her legs out of my way, so I stumbled over them as I made a beeline for the exit. I didn't stop until I pushed through the exit doors and the fresh air hit me.

The sun had set, leaving only a lingering glow in the sky. I let the door swing shut behind me as I leaned against the outside wall and closed my eyes. I took slow, deep breaths through my nose and out my mouth. I needed to calm down, or I was going to make a fool of myself.

I spread my hands open and pressed my palms to the

rough brick wall behind me. The jagged edges helped ground me in the present and bring my body back to equilibrium.

I could do this. I could be here in Harmony. I could face my mom and the town I grew up in. I could face...Jax.

It amazed me how out of place I felt in my hometown. Even though some things had changed, for the most part it was still Harmony. I should take comfort in that, but it felt as if my entire body was rejecting this place. All I could think about was going back home where I was safe.

Ten minutes passed, and I finally felt put together enough to go back inside. This time, I lingered in the back of the room, where I felt safe. Plus, when this whole thing was over, I was going to be the first out the door.

Elmore Phillips, the owner of Pop Hardware, the handyman store in town, was standing in the midst of the others, talking about how construction in Harmony was good for business. He didn't see the issue with the town getting a makeover. His words were not being received well. Betty Lou's lips were pinched so tight that their color had disappeared. But Elmore just kept on talking, seemingly oblivious to the daggers people were throwing his direction as they stared at him. When he finally finished and sat down, no one clapped or spoke. Everyone seemed to be stunned into silence.

"Thank you, Elmore. I'm happy these events have been favorable for you, but many of us don't see it that way," Betty said as she stood up. "At Godwins, our business has been in the family for generations. We're not interested in it being turned into a big chain grocery store."

The room erupted in applause. Elmore harrumphed and folded his arms across his chest. Mattie Monroe from Mattie's Antiques stood up and started talking about how even though the increased foot traffic was nice, she was conflicted about selling. The offer she'd received from Deveraux had been substantial, and she was looking to move back to Seattle to take care of her mother. There was a hushed whisper that rippled through the crowd of people wondering what that number had been.

I had to admit, I was curious as well. If this company was serious about buying up the whole town, they had to be shelling out a pretty penny. Someone from the audience shouted out for her to reveal the number, but Mattie's cheeks just reddened as she frowned and sat down.

"If Betty Lou asks, I've been here the entire time." A soft feminine voice drew my attention over. The woman looked my age. Her hair was wind-blown, and her cheeks were flushed like she'd rushed to get here. When I didn't answer her right away, she glanced over at me. She gave me a warm smile. "Are you new?"

I studied her. Was *I* new? I was fairly certain I should be the one asking her that. "Not new," I said as I straightened.

She frowned. "I haven't seen you around town."

Betty Lou was now standing and giving the group a lecture on how if everyone bands together, Deveraux

Construction won't be able to do anything. I turned to the woman standing next to me.

"I'm Claire," I said as I reached my hand out. "Missy's daughter."

Recognition passed over her face. "Oh, you're Missy's daughter?" she half said, half asked. I nodded. "How's your mom?"

I shoved my hands into the front pockets of my jeans. "She's okay. She's sent me here to represent her in this meeting."

The woman nodded as she glanced around the room.

"And you are?" I asked, leaning forward.

Her gaze whipped back to me. "Abigail. I run The Shop Around the Corner."

"Nice to meet you." It was nice to have someone here to talk to other than Rose and Jax—who I was currently forbidding myself from looking at.

"What did I miss?" Abigail asked. "I'm fairly certain that when Betty Lou finds me, she's going to quiz me."

"Some company called Deveraux Construction is wanting to buy the town and turn it into a destination for the wealthy."

Abigail nodded. "And where are people landing when it comes to selling?"

"Elmore and Mattie have spoken in favor. Everyone else seems to be against, but they also haven't seen the offers. From what Mattie said, the offers have been substantial."

Abigail had her focus on the ground as she listened.

When I finished, she glanced over at me. "And your mom is against this."

"Of course."

"Interesting," she said.

"What about you?"

Abigail grew quiet as her gaze scanned the room. When she finally turned back to me, she shrugged. "I'm not sure. I mean, I love my shop and this town, but traffic wasn't like this before all of the construction. If the offers are rejected, they will leave, taking all the customers with them. It's easy to reject offers when things are going well, but I fear that the town forgets what it was like before all of this business."

She did have a point. If Harmony Island was going to chase investors out of town, they needed to come up with something to bring guests here on a regular basis.

"But really, I'll go the direction the rest of the town feels is right." Elmore was now standing and shouting at Patty, the owner of the flower shop in town. "If they can actually come to a decision," Abigail said as she leaned closer to me.

I chuckled. That was going to be the struggle. Everyone in this town had their own opinions, and it was going to take a miracle for them all to come to a consensus.

Abigail stayed next to me for the rest of the meeting. The conversation slowly moved toward long-held grievances and away from what to do about Deveraux, so Betty Lou called the meeting to a close and everyone stood up from their seats. People lingered around the room, chatting and returning to the refreshment table.

I was waiting for Rose, who was currently talking to a few ladies from her sewing circle. I stayed near the door, but out of the way so that people didn't feel like they needed to talk to me.

Abigail was approached by a few shop owners I didn't recognize, so I put some distance between us, silently praying that Rose would finish her conversation so we could go. I was trying to ignore Jax, but he was slowly making his way around the room, and with every stride, he was getting closer and closer to me.

"You should stop by the shop sometime," Abigail said, breaking through my thoughts.

I glanced over at her. She looked genuine, so I returned the smile. "That would be nice. If I can get away, I'll try to stop by."

"What do you do?" she asked. "I mean, when you're not here in Harmony."

"I work at an animal shelter."

"Oh fun. When I was a kid, my dream was to work with animals."

"It has its struggles, but the pros outweigh the cons." A soft smile emerged as thoughts of the animals at the shelter flooded my mind. Sure, there had been tragic moments, but seeing a family take home an animal made it all worth it.

"So, if you always wanted to work with animals, how did you end up here, owning a bookstore?"

"Slash bakery."

I raised an eyebrow.

She chuckled. "The bakery keeps the business afloat right now."

"Ah."

She shrugged. "Life has a way of taking you down paths you never imagined. My aunt needed someone to take over, and I needed a job. And now, I'm here." She sighed. "And I haven't left."

"And you enjoy it?"

Her smile faltered, and a sense of sadness washed over her. Then she shook her head and glanced back over at me. "I do. It's what's right for me."

I wondered if she really believed that or if she was just saying the words in an effort to make them feel true. I decided not to push, so we returned our conversation to surface level. She asked me how long I planned on staying, and I replied that I hoped it wouldn't be too long. I left off the part about how my mother made my life miserable and just said that I had lots of work to return to.

Rose approached us and greeted Abigail. Jax was also headed our way, so I said a quick goodbye to Abigail, linked arms with Rose, and pulled her away before she engaged in yet another long conversation.

Rose was confused at first, protesting that she wanted to stay, but I shot her a look and she seemed to understand. We walked arm in arm to the car and climbed inside. Once we were on the road, I leaned my head back and took a few deep breaths.

"What did you think?" Rose asked, breaking the silence.

I tipped my head and glanced out the window. I wasn't sure what to say, so I just shrugged.

"You survived," Rose offered.

I studied her. "I survived."

She grinned at me. "And every day will get easier and easier until, eventually, you'll never want to leave and will stay here forever."

I snorted and moved my head until I was staring straight ahead. "That will never happen."

Rose's soft chuckle filled the air. "I have twenty bucks on you staying." She paused. "And I never lose."

10

BASH

"Sebastian."

Nicholas' sharp voice cut through my dreams, and I bolted up in bed. I was disoriented as I searched the room for the source of his voice. Had I been hallucinating? Thankfully, I found the dark form of Nicholas as he stood next to my bed. I wasn't going crazy.

I pushed up to sitting with one hand and leaned forward to turn on the light. "Nicholas," I said, my voice gruff from sleep, "what do you need?"

My question faded from my mind as I took in the solemn look on his face. I knew what was going on.

"Dad," I whispered.

Nicholas cleared his throat and nodded. "It's time to say goodbye."

I watched as he turned and walked from the room,

leaving me sitting on my bed, alone. I rested my arm on my knee as I stared out at my stark, cold room. Dad was leaving this world in a matter of moments, and I was going to be left here...alone.

Tears pricked my eyes, making me feel angry. I shouldn't cry over the death of that man. I was the reason he was so broken. He was going to the grave with the heartache that I caused him. I didn't have the right to feel sad.

My family was torn apart because of me.

I felt numb as I climbed out of bed and shuffled over to my dresser. I slipped on a pair of jeans and a black t-shirt before I headed into the bathroom and splashed some water on my face. Then I headed down the hallway and lingered outside of my father's door.

I could hear a soft, feminine voice that I could only assume was Emery's. She was speaking in a hushed tone, occasionally joined by a deep, masculine voice that I recognized as Dad's doctor. I pushed my hands through my hair as the war inside my chest raged.

I knew I should walk in there, but I didn't deserve to be in the presence of my family. Their lives had been irrevocably changed because of me. It was best for them if I just disappeared. If I left and never came back. Why did I think I should be here? My family was better off without me. I was sure of it.

"Come on." Nicholas appeared in front of me and grabbed my arm.

I inwardly thanked him as he pulled me into the room and pushed me over to my father's bed. The monitors were beeping so loud that it echoed in my head. My gaze drifted over to my father, who was still and pale. He looked as if he were peacefully sleeping.

"You need to say goodbye," Nicholas hissed in my ear as he pushed me closer.

My entire body rejected how close I was to my father, but I didn't pull back. Instead, I just stood there, staring down at my father's body. The room was quiet now. I could feel everyone's gaze on me. They were all waiting for me to do something, but I wasn't sure what that something was.

Should I cry? Let out a wail as I drop to my knees and grab my father's hand? That's what people did in the movies when someone they loved was about to pass away. They felt broken and unsure how they were going to continue their life without that person.

Why didn't I feel like that? My body felt cold, and there was nothing I could do to breathe life into it. I was frozen in a past I could never escape from. Nothing was going to bring me warmth to make my heart beat again. With Dad's death, I was now alone. My entire family was gone, and all that remained was me.

A hollow wail filled my ears. It wasn't the slow and steady beat I'd heard when I walked into the room. Now, it was just one solid sound. Movement around me drew my attention. The doctor that had been talking to Emery pushed past me and over to my dad. His fingers pressed to Dad's neck as he assessed the monitors around the bed.

Then he looked back to Nicholas and then to me.

"Your father is gone." His words sounded muffled. Like he was speaking to me underwater.

A priest that I hadn't noticed stepped up to the bed and began to speak. Emery stepped up next to me and stood there as we watched the nurses quietly turn off the monitors.

I didn't speak. I didn't know what I was going to say or what I was going to do. I just stood there, watching the last person in my family slip away from me.

"Bash?"

I blinked, hearing my name but not really knowing where to look.

"Sebastian."

I turned to see Nicholas staring at me. I wasn't sure if he wanted me to speak, but I knew I couldn't. My heart was breaking in a way that I hadn't expected—I didn't have the right to feel this way.

"Are you okay?" he asked. I could see the concern in his gaze, and I hated it.

"I...um..." I took a step back. The walls felt like they were closing in on me. I couldn't breathe. I couldn't think. My body yelled at me to get the hell out of this room.

No one stopped me as I turned and headed straight for the exit. Once I was in the hallway, I allowed my feet to take over as I hurried to my room and shut the door. Now alone, I leaned against the door and closed my eyes, tipping my face toward the ceiling.

Breathe.

I hated that I was here. I hated that I was now alone. But the thing that I hated the most was that I was never going to be able to make this up to my father. He was gone. Carson was gone. Mom was gone. And I was the only one left alive.

I straightened and pushed off the door. I crossed the room and grabbed my phone. It was charging on the night-stand. The blue glow of the screen filled the room as I waited for the camera to recognize my face. I found my text messages and scrolled until I saw Anders' name.

He was the only person I had left. There was no way I could do the funeral arrangements alone. Nicholas was here, but he was a constant reminder of who I had lost. If I was going to make it through this, I needed my friend here.

Me: My dad just passed away. I could use a friend.

My fingers felt numb as I punched out each letter and finally sent it off. Then I collapsed back on my bed and closed my eyes. I was now the owner of Torres Investments. My life was fundamentally changing, and I was not ready for it.

My phone chimed. I dropped my hand and patted the bed next to me, looking for it. The cool material brushed my fingers, and I picked it up, holding it above my head so I could read the message.

Anders: You've got it man. I'll head up in the morning.

I sent a thumbs-up emoji and then dropped my phone

back onto the bed. I grabbed a nearby pillow, set it over my face, and took a deep breath.

Anders was coming. It wasn't ideal, but it was what I needed for now.

I was going to try to get some sleep, and in the morning, I was going to face my future and whatever that entailed.

11

ABIGAIL

SWEET TEA & SOUTHERN GENTLEMAN

The smell of chocolate chip muffins filled the bookstore. I inhaled, closing my eyes. My mouth watered.

"I told you I was right," Dad said as he appeared next to me carrying the muffin tin in his oven-mitted hand. "It's your grandfather's recipe that he passed down to me, and now I get to pass it down to you." He waggled his finger in my direction as he walked past to set down the muffin tin.

"I shouldn't have doubted you," I said as I moved to lean against the counter, watching him as he gingerly plucked them from the tin and set them on the cooling rack.

He'd left Sabrina and me when Mom died, and we'd gone years without speaking, but I was glad we'd been able to move past the pain. Well, I'd moved past faster than Sabrina, but she was coming around to him. Especially since he and Penny were staying in Harmony for the foreseeable future. It was starting to feel like we were a family again.

"I like her," I said as I picked up my mug of coffee and inhaled.

Dad looked at me from over his glasses. "Like who?"

"Penny." I took a sip.

A soft, lovesick smile spread across Dad's lips. "Oh," he said as he pulled the last muffin from the tin and straightened. "Yeah, I like her too."

"Is she liking her time here in Harmony?"

He nodded. "She misses Maggie and the babies, but she's enjoying getting to know you girls and Samuel."

Gratitude rose up inside of me. I loved Maggie, and I knew what it was like to miss your mother. But I was grateful that she was sharing her family with us and that Penny cared enough to stay.

"Well, Maggie will have to come down here and stay sometime," I offered just as the second oven's timer beeped. I grabbed a nearby mitt and pulled open the door. The smell of melted chocolate blasted me, making my mouth water once more. I pulled out the muffins and brought them over to Dad, who was taking a sip of his coffee.

"I'll tell her that," he said as he set his mug down before pulling the muffins out of the tin.

I grabbed the muffin liners to refill the emptied tins just as a frantic knock sounded on the front door. I glanced up to see Shelby in a pair of yoga pants and a t-shirt with a small brown-and-white dog attached to a leash. Her hair was wild, and it matched the crazed look in her gaze. I dropped the muffin cups onto the counter and hurried over.

I unlocked the door and pushed it open. "Shelby? What are you doing? It's your honeymoon." I pointed down at the small dog. Its ribs were showing, and its tail was tucked between its legs. "And that's a dog."

Shelby nodded. "I know. I'm so sorry to bother you, but Miles and I finally discovered what's been scratching at my door. This poor girl is starving." Her gaze met mine as she winced. "Is there any way you could take her? The shelter isn't open, and Dr. Orinz isn't answering. I'm not sure what to do with her, but we can't have her at the inn because of allergies and such."

I gave her a comforting smile. "I'll take care of her," I said as she slipped the leash into my hand.

She looked relieved. "Thank you. If it wasn't..." She waved her hand around.

"Go back to Miles. It's your honeymoon. Have fun. I'll take care of this."

She grinned at me and then turned and hurried over to Miles' truck. She gave me a quick wave and then pulled away from the street and disappeared in the direction of the inn.

For a moment, a stab of jealousy pummeled my chest. I was happy for my friend, but it was hard when my own love life was so strange. I just hoped, one day, I would have a man to drive home to that fast.

I glanced down to see the dog sitting next to me. She was shaking and lifting her paws up off the ground. I glanced around, not knowing what I was going to do with this animal. I'd offered to take it off of Shelby's hands, but I was at work...in a bakery. A dog couldn't come in.

I glanced up and down the street. There was no way I could leave her out here. After all, she was terrified. But the last thing I needed was for the county to find out that I had an animal inside of my shop. I led it around the building and to the backdoor, where she would have some shade.

I tied her leash to one of the parking posts by the door, told her I would be right back, and then pulled open the back door and entered.

"Dad?" I called out. I stopped at the sink and washed my hands before I made my way further into the shop.

"Yeah, Abby?" He appeared from the front.

I dug around in the back for an old mixing bowl. "I have a dog now."

He frowned. "A dog?"

I nodded as I pulled out a bowl and blew off the dust. Then I stuck it under the faucet. Water began filling the bowl. "Shelby dropped her by. So now I need to figure out what to do with her." The bowl was full, so I turned off the faucet and picked up the bowl with both hands.

Dad followed me to the back door and pulled it open for me. The dog was sitting next to the post, and when I approached, she stood and pulled back. I could see the fear on her face. I set the bowl down and stepped back. "Shelby said that Dr. Orinz isn't in yet, so I can't take her to the vet." I glanced over at Dad, who looked as confused as I felt.

"My apartment doesn't allow dogs. And she can't stay

here." I tapped my chin. Suddenly, the conversation I had
last night with Claire popped into my mind. "I wonder..."

"What?"

I headed back into the store and over to my office to grab
my purse and keys.

"Where are you going?" Dad asked as he followed me.

I slung my purse up onto my shoulder. "Can you open
the store? I have to run to the Apple Blossom B&B. I'll be
right back, I promise."

Dad nodded as he kept pace with me as I walked back to
the dog. She was lapping up the water, but as soon as we
approached, she pulled back again. I untied her leash and
then looped it a few times around my hand. Thankfully, she
was okay with being led, so I brought her over to my car and
got her situated in the back seat. "I'll be back," I called over
my shoulder as I pulled open the driver's door.

The drive to the B&B wasn't too long. I pulled up the
long driveway and parked in the back. I kept the dog in the
car as I got out and headed over to the porch. I climbed up
the stairs, and when I got to the front door, I paused, not
sure if I should walk in or not.

How stupid, this was a B&B. I turned the door handle
and pushed inside. The ceiling in the foyer was tall. A set of
stairs stretched out in the middle of the room and then
turned and went up either direction. A small desk was off to
the side, so I stepped up to it and rang the little bell resting
on top.

The sound reverberated in the room, and I waited for

someone to respond. My phone buzzed in my purse, star-tling me. When I pulled it out, I saw I had a text from Anders. I swiped up and read the first few lines.

Anders: I need to leave town for a few days. Bash texted and he—

"Can I help you?"

My heart took off racing as I quickly shoved my phone back into my purse like I'd been caught doing something I shouldn't. Claire had entered from one of the back hallways. Her hair was pulled up into a ponytail, and she wore a tattered shirt. She was carrying a bucket in one of her gloved hands.

"Abigail?" she asked as she moved closer, like I was the last person she expected to see standing in the foyer.

"Hey." I forced my thoughts away from Anders' text and whatever he was going to tell me about Bash and focused my attention on Abigail and the dog currently sitting in the back of my car.

"What's wrong?" Claire set down the bucket and pulled off her gloves.

I waved away her concern. "Nothing to panic about," I said.

She stepped up to the desk and set her gloves down. "You look like you've just seen a ghost."

I took a deep breath and shook my head. "Sorry. I was just reading a text when you startled me."

Her gaze dropped down to my purse. I hooked my

thumb around the strap and shook my head. "It's fine. It's all good. It's nothing you or I need to worry about."

She eyed me for a moment. "So, what are you doing here at the Apple Blossom? Did something happen with that construction company? Dever-something?"

I shook my head again. "I'm actually not sure. I'm here because a dog was dropped off on my doorstep. But my apartment doesn't allow dogs, and I can't keep her at my store because..." I sucked in my breath. "The whole food and dogs situation."

Claire's face relaxed, and a sparkle I hadn't seen last night flashed in her eyes. She nodded. "A dog? Of course." Then she glanced around. "Do you have her here?"

I waved for her to follow me as I started walking toward the front door. "She's in my car."

"Hang on." Claire held up her finger and tipped her head toward the stairs, calling up, "I'll be right back, Rose."

There was a muffled response, and then Rose appeared at the top of the stairs. "What?" When her gaze landed on me, she smiled. "Hey, Abigail."

"Abigail has a dog in her car that she wants me to take a look at. I'll be right back." Claire motioned for me to keep walking.

"A wha—"

Claire shut the door before Rose could finish her question. "So where did you find it?"

I motioned toward the car that I could just barely see

from around the corner of the house. Claire kept pace with me.

"Shelby found it down at the Harmony Inn."

Claire suddenly stopped in her tracks. Her hand reached out and grabbed my arm. I stopped as well, shocked that she would have this kind of reaction. "Did you say Shelby's at the Harmony Inn?"

I nodded, suddenly remembering that Shelby had a history with this family. I felt ridiculous for having brought her up. Did Shelby want the whole Willis family to know that she was back and living at the inn? "Yeah," I finally let out once it became clear that Claire wasn't going to let me go until I responded.

"She's back in town? Since when?"

"After her grandmother died."

"Her grandmother *died?*"

I felt like I was betraying Shelby's confidence, and I feared what else I would tell Claire if I kept going. "The dog's probably getting pretty hot," I said as I crossed the gravel lot and pulled open the back door to my car. Hopefully, changing the subject would keep me from spilling any more secrets.

"Oh, she's so sweet!" Claire was next to me with her hands extended. The dog didn't seem as bothered with Claire as she'd been with me. She let Claire cup her face in her hands and even tried licking her a few times.

Claire ran her hands down the length of the dog's body

and glanced up at me. "She's thin, that's for sure. But I think that's all." She stopped and glanced up like she was trying to feel something. "Well, that and the ticks."

My skin began to crawl at the mention of those parasites. The strong urge to get the dog out of my car filled me. Thankfully, Claire called for the dog to follow her and stepped out of the way so the dog could jump down.

There must be something about Claire because the dog that emerged was not the same dog I'd packed into the car ten minutes ago. Her tail was wagging, and she was threading herself in and out of Claire's legs. Claire was laughing, all the while keeping her hand down toward the dog's face so she could lick her.

"I think she'll be okay here," Claire said as she smiled up at me. She kept herself hunched forward as if she were refusing to break her connection with the dog.

"You sure? It'll just be until we can get her another place to stay," I reassured her, but Claire waved my words away.

"My mom won't be back for a week. So she can stay here until we figure something out."

I grinned. "Wonderful! Well, just let me know if you need any help with anything. Food, toys, etc." I pulled my keys from my purse.

"I will! I'll see you later?" Claire asked as the dog began to pull her toward the house.

I nodded. "Definitely."

She rounded the house and disappeared, so I headed

over to my car and pulled open the door. As I climbed in, I set my purse down on the passenger seat and started the engine. I paused, glancing over at my purse.

The start of Anders' text looped through my mind like a skipping CD. Why was he telling me about Bash? What did it matter? He'd gone home. He was rich now. Whatever reason he'd had for being in Harmony must have disappeared. I was probably the last person he was thinking about, which meant he was the last person I should be thinking about.

I put the car into reverse and pulled out of the parking lot and down the driveway. I wasn't going to rush to read Anders' text. I didn't really care what he had to say about Bash. It was only going to mess with my mind.

By the time I pulled into the back parking lot at the shop, I'd successfully pushed Anders and his text about Bash from my mind. The dog had been dropped off, Dad had opened the shop, and I was going to move forward with my original plan of forgetting Bash and all of our confusing interactions.

I slipped my keys into my purse and pulled open the back door. I could hear voices coming from inside the store as I set my purse down in the office, grabbed an apron, and headed out into the store. My whole body stopped when I glanced up and saw Anders standing there, talking to Dad. They were laughing like they'd known each other for years and were just catching up.

APPLE BLOSSOM B&B   121

"Hey," I said cautiously as I approached.

"You're back," Dad said as he wrapped his arm around my shoulders. "I was just getting to know your *boyfriend*."

I glared at him, and he just chuckled.

"I didn't know you were dating someone is all I'm saying," he said as he raised his hands in surrender.

"You can see now why I kept my family a secret," I said as I walked over to Anders and gave him a quick kiss. His arm found my waist and he pulled me against him.

"I was just telling your dad that I wanted to whisk you away for a few days."

I turned to face him. "You want to what?"

He met my gaze. "I texted you. Did you not get it?"

I chewed my lip, recounting the very detailed thought process I went through to avoid reading his text. It seemed as if I was going to have to face it no matter what. "I didn't," I lied.

Anders turned to face me. "Sebastian's dad passed away, and he asked me to come up there. I was thinking you might want to join me."

My heart ached at the news that Bash had lost a parent. But that didn't mean I wanted to go visit him. To see him again.

"Sebastian...why does that name sound familiar?" Dad asked.

"He's Anders' friend," I said quickly.

Dad shook his head. And then, like a lightbulb went off

in his head, his eyes widened. "He's the man that found Sabrina."

I felt Anders stiffen next to me. It was a sore subject for Anders, and I preferred just moving on from it. "That's right."

"Well then you have to go."

I stared at Dad. He was joking, right? "But I have the shop to run."

Dad shook his head. "I can do it. I'm having fun. And Fanny will be in later to take over." He began to walk toward us. "You two go. He helped your sister; go help him grieve his father. It's the least you can do."

I sputtered, but Dad didn't stop to listen. And Anders seemed happy to guide me out of the shop at my father's bidding. Finally, I got my bearings enough to turn around and hold up my hand. "Wait!"

Both men stopped and turned to look at me.

I was frustrated that I hadn't had any time to process what was happening, and yet, the only thing I could think was that I needed my purse.

"I'll be right back," I tossed over my shoulder as I headed toward my office.

Once I was alone, I shut the door and leaned against it. My heart was racing as I tipped my head back and closed my eyes. All of the positive thinking that I'd done on the ride over here was for naught. My entire body was flushed with the idea that I was going to see Bash.

I'd sworn to myself that I was never going to talk to Bash again. Or even think about him. And now? Now, in less than a car ride to New York, I was going to see him. I was nowhere near prepared for this.

Crap.

12

BASH

SWEET TEA & SOUTHERN GENTLEMAN

It had been twenty-four hours since Dad died, and I thought by now I would have cried. But I couldn't seem to bring on any tears. Instead, I was just going through the motions.

Thankfully, I had Nicholas here to help me take care of things, and Dad had been very specific in his will as to how he wanted his funeral and burial to go, so it seemed like I was just here as a formality.

People from the funeral home came to the house. I sat with the director as he told me what Dad had requested. I just nodded along with everything he said and signed a few papers, and they left. The hollow sound of the door closing on this big empty house marking their departure.

Emery came by for a few of the meetings, but she kept her distance from me. After everything was finished, she left without saying goodbye. Emmeline offered to help, but I just told her that I wanted to handle this on my own. She seemed to understand and told me she was here to help when I needed her.

I was alone. Nicholas left to meet with the florist. He had a chef come in to cook me meals for the next week. Even the maid who cleaned the house had finished her work and left an hour ago.

The house was quiet, and it was making my skin crawl. I needed something to distract me. Someone to talk to. Something to break up this deafening silence. Even though I was in a mansion, I felt like the walls were caving in on me.

I walked into the living room and grabbed the remote. I turned on the surround system and a robotic voice asked me what I wanted to listen to. I selected the greatest hits from Imagine Dragons, and as soon as the songs started up, I told it to play at max volume, and the music blared from the speakers.

I made my way into the kitchen, and the lights automatically turned on. I told them to dim to half as I wandered over to the fridge and pulled it open. I grabbed out one of the pre-portioned meals and opened it up. It was a slab of meat with some potatoes all drizzled with gravy. I slipped it into the microwave.

A rich man's TV dinner.

I leaned against the counter and tipped my head back, closing my eyes. The music that blared from the speakers reverberated in my chest, and I hummed along with the words. The stress that had clung to my muscles all day was starting to dissipate.

A loud buzzing noise drew me back to reality. I straightened and glanced around, wondering if I'd just imagined it. The intercom next to the garage door was the culprit, so I walked over to it. The button next to *Front Gate* was blinking.

"Hello?"

"Bash?"

Anders. "You made it," I said as I pressed the button to open the gate, and a smile spread across my lips. Finally. Some sense of normalcy was headed my way.

I grabbed out another dinner from the fridge and set it on the counter as I waited for him to pull up to the house. I turned down the music so I could hear him knock. When the sound echoed in the foyer, I left what I was doing in the kitchen and headed out to the door. As soon as I pulled it open and saw Anders standing there, I pulled him into a hug.

"I'm so glad you could make it," I said when I pulled back.

Anders grinned back at me. "I'm glad you asked."

I stepped away from the door so he could enter. "How was your trip?"

"Long." He reached down and grabbed the two suitcases next to him. "We were ready to get out of the car."

"I bet," I said as I held the door for him. He stepped into the foyer, and just as he moved past me, his words washed over me once more. "Did you say *we?*"

Before he could answer, my entire body turned numb as

Abigail appeared in front of me. She looked nervous as she met my gaze and then dropped it only to look back up at me. "Hey, Bash," she whispered.

All I could do was stare at her. I knew I wasn't dreaming —all of my dreams about Abigail most certainly didn't include Anders—she was really standing here. In my father's house. Staring up at me.

"Abigail?" I barely managed out.

"Yeah, sorry," Anders apologized. "I should have texted. But I asked Abby to come with me."

"Abby?" I knew I should drop my gaze. That it wasn't right for me to be staring at my best friend's girl. But I couldn't believe she was here. I also couldn't believe that she looked more beautiful than I remembered; it had only been a few days.

Anders appeared next to her and slipped his arm around her waist. It might have been my imagination, my desire for her to want me instead of him, but I swore she tensed from his touch. And I hated myself for thinking that. For wanting that.

"I hope it's okay that I tagged along," Abigail said, her voice soft as she met my gaze.

Knowing I couldn't stand in the foyer with the door open, staring at my friend's girlfriend, I nodded. "Of course. I've got plenty of room."

"I'd say," Anders said as he left Abigail's side so he could walk further into the house.

Abigail's hand went to her elbow as if she were trying to

contain her body heat. I watched her, still shocked that she was even here. Why *was* she here?

"Of all the years I've known you, you could have hinted that this was your life." Anders turned his attention to me.

"This isn't my life," I said quickly. "This is my father's life."

Anders studied me for a moment before he shrugged. "Still. You could have at least hinted that you were the famed Torres son."

I didn't want to talk about my past. The last thing I wanted was to talk about Carson—I certainly didn't want Abigail to know what I'd done. I couldn't handle the disappointed look I knew would flash in her eyes when I told her that I was responsible for my brother's death.

I wasn't sure I could come back from that. It was hard enough with Emery.

"I was making some dinner, if you guys are hungry," I said as I started to make my way through the foyer and over to the kitchen. Anders followed me, but Abigail just stood there like she wasn't sure what she was supposed to do with the suitcases. "I can show you to your rooms later."

Abigail's gaze met mine, and my heart began to pound. She didn't look away. Instead, she held my gaze as if she were assessing my words. Then she slowly walked toward me.

Anders was already in the kitchen, so I waited for Abigail to pass by before I followed after her. I could smell the sweet honey scent of her shampoo and reveled in the feeling of being this close to her.

I both hated and loved that she was here. This was a beautiful sort of torture. On the one hand, I wanted her in Harmony, living her life and falling in love. On the other hand, I was selfish. I wanted to see her face, hear her voice, and love her.

When she was here, I could pretend that she was mine. And right now, that was enough. My life had felt so dark for so long, and the only light was Abigail. I wasn't ready to snuff that out now that it was standing right next to me, watching me pull another dinner from the fridge.

"Filet mignon?" Anders asked as he slid the container of food toward himself and studied the top.

I shrugged. "They left me a lot of different things," I said as I popped off the top and slipped it into the microwave.

"They?"

I paused and glanced over at Abigail and Anders before focusing on starting the microwave. "My dad's chef."

Anders let out a low whistle. "I can't believe we were slumming it in our apartment when you had this to live in."

I stared at the microwave door as the contents spun in a circle. Why wouldn't Anders just let this go? This was my dad's house. It was my dad's chef. It was my dad's money. None of this was mine. Even though I was his heir and was about to inherit the Torres fortune, that didn't make any of this mine. But I didn't know how to say those things without him asking questions, so I decided to just keep quiet.

Thankfully, Abigail kept the conversation light as we ate. I stayed standing next to the counter while Anders and Abigail sat at the bar on the far side of the island. From where I was, I could tilt my body so that Abigail was just out of my sight, and I was using that to my advantage, especially when she spoke.

They told me what was going on at Harmony and how the store owners were gathering together to fight Deveraux Construction and keep them from buying up all the property.

I listened in silence. With all the chaos around my father's passing, I'd completely forgotten about Emmeline's plans for Harmony. I wondered if I should say something about it to Abigail and Anders but decided against it. At least for now.

Anders finished his food and stretched back on the barstool, rubbing his stomach as he glanced around. Then he yawned before looking back at me. "I'm beat. I could use a nap."

I set my dish in the sink. I was only about halfway finished, but I wasn't really hungry. I nodded as I turned on the faucet and rinsed the food down the sink. "Yeah, I can show you to a guest room."

"You mean rooms."

I glanced over at Abigail, who was moving to stand. "Rooms," I repeated. I wanted to ask why she wasn't staying with Anders but decided against it.

We walked through the kitchen and out to the foyer,

where Anders grabbed his bag. I reached down to get Abigail's at the same time she reached to pick it up. Our fingers brushed, and heat mixed with electricity raced through my body from her touch.

My gaze snapped to hers, and she looked as startled as I felt before she suddenly pulled her hands back and gripped them against her chest. "Sorry," she whispered.

I shook my head. "That was my fault."

She didn't look up at me again. Instead, she turned and took a few steps away from me. I hoisted the luggage up and motioned with my head for them to follow me up the stairs.

When we got to the first guest room, I shifted the bag until my fingers were free to grasp the door handle. Anders was the first to walk through the door, and as soon as he did, he dropped his luggage on the floor and collapsed face-first on the bed, spreading his legs and arms out like a starfish.

"This feels so good," he moaned into the down comforter.

I chuckled as I walked through the room to the bathroom and flipped on the light. "It has its own bathroom."

"With a jacuzzi?" Anders' voice grew loud as he appeared next to me. He entered the bathroom and stared down at the eight-jetted tub against the wall. "Babe, come look at this!"

My skin crawled at the way he called Abigail, *Babe*. I wanted to think that she didn't enjoy that either, which is why she didn't rush over. A few seconds passed before she was standing next to me.

I tried not to, but I dropped my gaze to watch her. She lingered for a moment before she stepped past me into the bathroom. "That looks amazing."

Anders whooped as he leaned forward and engaged the plug before turning the faucet on. Then he straightened and started to pull off his shirt. "I'm taking a bath. You can join me if you want," he said with a wink in Abigail's direction.

Not wanting to watch the two of them flirt, I ducked my head and left the room. Once I was out in the hallway, I took a deep breath. Maybe Abigail had misspoke downstairs about wanting a separate room.

I turned and started down the hallway, ready to hide away in my room. Being out here just made the reality of the two of them being together that much more poignant.

"Bash?"

My entire body froze from the sound of my name on Abigail's lips. I stared straight ahead, wanting to keep moving. But I knew I was going to turn to face her. No matter where she was in her life, if she needed me, I was going to be there. I took in a deep breath and slowly turned to face her.

I dragged my gaze up to meet hers, my heart pounding so hard I could hear it in my ears. She was studying me when my gaze finally settled on her. Her eyebrows were drawn together like she had so many questions but didn't know where to start.

"Can you show me my room?" she asked quietly.

I glanced toward Anders' bedroom to see that the door

had been shut. "Are you..." My voice trailed off as the real-ization of what I was about to ask washed over me. Why did I care? I shouldn't be asking her if she was going to take a bath with my friend. That was none of my business.

Abigail's cheeks heated as she glanced toward the door and then back to me. She shook her head. "I think he can bathe on his own." Her shoulders sagged, and I could see that she was exhausted.

The sudden urge to take care of her washed over me, and it was taking all of my strength not to walk over to her, pick her up, and carry her to the other guest room.

Feeling like an idiot and fighting the urge to just take over the rational part of my brain and act, I shoved my hands into the front pockets of my pajama pants. "So, you want me to show you the other guest room?"

"Yes, please," she said.

She started to bend down to pick up her luggage, but I beat her to it. She took a step back as if my presence was repulsive to her.

"I can do that," she whispered.

I shook my head. "Not in my house." I didn't wait for her response before I headed down the hallway toward my room. Sure, there were guest rooms closer to Anders, but I wanted her near to me. It was ridiculous, but I was tired of fighting reality. For now, I was going to keep her close so I could keep her safe.

I could hear Abigail's footfalls behind me as she followed. When I got to the room, she didn't let me open the door for her. She reached out and turned the handle then waited for me to go in first before following after.

I walked in and set the luggage down by the dresser on the far wall. With my hands free and having no other reason to be in her room, I turned to leave. She was lingering near the door with her hands clasped in front of her as she looked around. "Your house is beautiful," she said softly as her gaze swept the room one more time before returning to me.

I pushed my hands through my hair, hating how raw I felt with her around. "It's my dad's house," I said dryly.

She slipped her beautiful bottom lip in between her teeth as she studied me. I could feel the questions in her gaze, and I both wanted them and feared them at the same time.

"Well, I'll leave you alone to rest," I said as I started walking toward the door.

Just as I passed by her, I felt her hand land on my arm.

"Bash," she whispered.

I fought an audible groan. I wanted to feel her touch again. The hug we shared outside of her broken-down car still haunted me. I wanted her pressed to my chest, her body wrapped in my arms. I wanted to respond, but I feared what I might say, so I just looked down at her.

"Why didn't you tell me that you found Sabrina?" Her gaze was focused on my chest, and then slowly, agonizingly slowly, she lifted it to meet mine.

My breathing turned shallow as I stared into her rich brown eyes. She was mere inches away from me. The heat between us rose, causing my skin to crackle from electricity. She wanted me to give her a reason why I would save her sister, but I didn't know how to say the truth. "Because you were scared."

Her lips parted. I wondered if she understood what those words really meant. *Because I'm falling in love with you.*

"But—"

I pulled my arm away and stepped back. "What do you want from me, Abigail? Why are you even here?"

She pulled back as if my words had smacked her across the face. I hated that she looked hurt, but I didn't know how to be friends with a woman I wanted the way I wanted Abigail. I'd moved away from Harmony. I was here to fix what I'd broken. And I hated that Abigail was now swept up in all of this.

"I needed to say thank you," she finally whispered.

"For finding Sabrina?"

She nodded.

"Consider me thanked," I said and then turned and left the room. I shut the door to make sure that she wasn't going to follow me. I didn't stop moving until I was in my room with my own door shut behind me.

I walked into my bathroom and slammed my fists down on the vanity. I tipped my head back and cursed, hating that my life was so messed up and there was nothing I could do to fix it.

Carson was gone. Emery was hurting. My dad was dead

and had left me with some decree that I marry Emmeline. That was hard enough. Adding Abigail into the mix was a torture that I was certain they saved for the seventh circle of hell.

I was being punished, fine. I could deal with that. But I couldn't stand seeing Abigail hurt. And one thing was for sure, the longer she stayed around me, the greater the chance of her getting hurt. I couldn't have that.

Not now. Not ever.

My job was to protect her. Even if it meant hurting myself, I would gladly sacrifice my happiness for hers. I would save her from the pain that only I seemed capable of giving.

And that started with staying far, *far* away from her.

13

CLAIRE

SWEET TEA & SOUTHERN GENTLEMAN

I screamed as Carmel shook, spraying me with soapy water. I leapt to the side to avoid the shower of droplets, but I wasn't fast enough, and I ended up with the front of my t-shirt soaking wet.

Rose chuckled. She was sitting on the front porch of the B&B, sipping lemonade and pretending not to watch me. She was aghast that I'd agreed to watch the dog and remained an ever-present observer, eyeing me as I attempted to feed and clean the dog I affectionately named Carmel.

"Your mother will lose her mind when she finds out that you allowed a dog on the grounds of her B&B," Rose had muttered under her breath yesterday as I filled bowls with water and meat scraps from the fridge.

I'd just shrugged. My mother hated me already, so I wasn't losing out on anything. An animal needed my help, and I wasn't going to walk away.

"You could help me," I called up to Rose as I stalked around Carmel, determined to scrub her down. The dog just watched me warily.

"And look like you? No, thank you." Rose raised her glass of lemonade, and the sound of ice clinking made my parched throat ache.

I shot her an annoyed look, but as I did, Carmel took her chance at freedom and sprinted across the yard. I yelped, stumbling to get my feet under me, and took off after her.

"Carmel!" I yelled as my flip-flops slipped on the grass. I had half a mind to kick them off, but there were too many jagged rocks around for me to trust that I wouldn't end up with cut up feet. I cursed as she took off into the brush at the edge of the woods around the B&B.

Mom owned the twenty acres that surrounded the B&B to keep a secluded feeling even though the building was located just a stone's throw from town. Normally, I didn't mind how intimate the grounds felt with the tall trees and thick brush, but it was going to be hell to find that dog.

"Carmel!" I shouted again, pushing through the brush, searching for any hint of Carmel's direction. I sighed as sweat pricked my neck and back. I was hot and irritated. I'd spent the last twenty minutes trying to clean her, and now all of my hard work was going to be for naught.

If she heard me, she didn't move to obey. All I could spot was some rustling in the woods, so I followed after it, praying that I was following Carmel and not some rabbit or squirrel.

I used to roam these woods as a kid. If I remembered right, there was a small pond somewhere back here that I'd follow my brothers to and beg them to let me fish with them.

Maybe that's where Carmel was headed to. Sweat was dripping down my back, and my thirst had been amplified from the humidity and exertion. She was still covered in her winter coat, so she had to be hotter than I was in my t-shirt and biker shorts.

Just as I pushed through a dense thicket of bushes, bright-blue shimmering water blinded me. I glanced down, making sure to judge where the shoreline was as I started creating a path in the long grass that grew around the pond.

"Carmel!" I called again, searching the water's edge for that ridiculous dog. "Where are you, you silly animal?" I huffed under my breath as I pushed away the branches of some unruly bushes that were stretching out in my path.

Suddenly, a man popped up from an especially thick patch of bushes that were growing right next to the pond just a few feet away from me. I screamed and stumbled forward, the front of my flip-flop catching on a root. I reached my hands out to stop my fall, but two arms wrapped around my waist, and suddenly I was pulled to his chest.

My heart raced as I whipped around, trying to see his face. I pushed at his arms in an effort to break his hold on me. If I was going to be murdered in the woods today, I was going to at least put up a fight.

"Will you wait just a second?"

Jax's familiar voice filled my ears, and my entire body stiffened when realization hit me. "Jax?" I whispered.

My feet touched solid ground before his arms released me. I steadied myself as Jax took a step back. I peeked over to see him pull his ball cap off his head and tousle his hair before he replaced it.

"What are you doing down here?" he asked as I slowly turned around.

I stared at him. "What are *you* doing down here?"

He glanced toward the water and then back to me before he squinted his eyes. "I didn't think anyone came down here anymore."

He hadn't answered my question. "Do you come here a lot?"

He started to walk back down to the water's edge. That's when I saw a fishing pole leaning against a three-legged stool.

"You're fishing?"

He grabbed at the fishing line attached to his pole and proceeded to place a worm on the hook. "Fishing relaxes me," he said before he dropped the hook and picked up the fishing pole. Then he pulled the tip of the pole back and cast the hook into the water before settling down on his stool.

"Does my mom know that you come here?" I knew the answer to that question before the words left my lips. I knew how Mom felt about Jax. She disliked him. Immensely. I was never really clear as to why. I thought it had something to do with an old family feud, but Mom had never gone into detail about what that feud might have been.

He glanced over at me for a second before returning his gaze to the water. "Are you going to tattle on me?"

I stared at him. That was not what I meant. "No." I wrapped my arm around my stomach, the wet shirt shocking my skin. That's when I remembered what I must look like. I reached up and raked my loose hair back into my ponytail, praying that I didn't look like a wet dog even though I felt— and smelled—like one.

"Do you do this a lot?" I asked, knowing that I should leave him alone to find Carmel. But for some reason, I couldn't get my feet to move. I glanced around, trying to see if I could spot that blasted dog. But I kept myself close enough so I could hear Jax. His responses intrigued me. Was he unhappy with his life? Did he...miss me?

"Only when I'm stressed." He paused. "Which happens more and more now."

"YOU'RE STRESSED?" Pained worry shot through my gut as I stopped to look at him. What was he stressed about?

He jerked his pole a few times, the water rippling around the spot where his hook was at. "Are you not stressed?" He glanced over at me, his gaze meeting mine, which caused my heart to pound.

The truth was, yes, I was stressed. Everything about my life was stressful. I'd thought that moving away from

Harmony and finding my own path would bring me happiness...but it hadn't. I was just as lonely and miserable in Florida as I was when I'd left here.

"I am," I whispered. "I don't think I know what it's like *not* to be stressed."

"Do you mean you didn't find happiness wherever it was you landed?" He grabbed the water bottle next to him and took a long drink.

"Florida, and no."

He studied me as he twisted the cap back onto the bottle. Then he set it down next to him and returned to his pole. "Wanna fish?" He held out his pole but didn't turn his gaze to look at me. Instead, he kept it focused on the water.

I knew I should say no. I knew I should just walk away and return to my quest to find Carmel, but I didn't. I didn't want to leave. So, I reached out and wrapped my fingers around the pole. Then I slid my hand down to its base and rested my hand on the reel.

I began to spin the handle and watched as the water rippled around the line.

"Who were you calling to earlier?" He squinted up at me.

I continued reeling in the line. "My dog. She got away from me while I was trying to give her a bath."

He chuckled. "Your mom let you bring a dog with you?"

I shook my head. The hook was midway up my pole, so I flipped the release and pulled the tip of the pole back so I could cast it into the water again. "No. Abigail brought her to me." I let the hook fly, and it landed in the middle of the pond. I returned the release and rested the butt of the pole against my hip.

"You're making friends fast," he said as he removed his cap once more and ruffled his hair.

"We met at the town hall."

He nodded. "I saw."

My cheeks heated. He'd been watching me? My heart picked up speed, and I feared that he could hear it. I cleared my throat and shifted my weight, moving ever so slightly away from him.

"So, what are your plans here?"

I glanced around. "To fish?"

He chuckled. It was low and soft, and my entire body was washed with the memory of what it had been like to be with him. I had so many questions to ask. Did he think about me? Did he miss me? Was it as hard for him to be around me as it was for me to be in his presence?

I pinched my lips together, hoping that it would remind me to not ask him any of those questions. It wasn't my right. I'd walked away. I'd broken his heart. I'd told him that we couldn't work.

I'd been tired of my family and my mom, and fear overtook me.

And when I'd overheard him laughing with his friends about all the things he was going to do once he got out of "this damn town," I ran. I wasn't proud of it, but I'd wanted to break his heart before he pulverized mine.

To see him still living here after all of these years confused me.

"I meant, here in Harmony." He glanced over at me once more. "I'm guessing you're not here to stay."

I studied him for a moment before the intensity grew too strong and I had to look away. "No. I'm just here to help Mom with the B&B while she recovers, and then I'm going to leave."

From the corner of my eye, I saw him drop his gaze back to the water.

"You're going to leave," he repeated, his voice low.

I wanted to ask him why he cared. I felt judged when I was around him. Like I was under a microscope as he searched for the happiness I'd declared I would find the night I walked away. I'd told him to watch me. I would leave Harmony and find the success I was never going to find here. He'd just stood there, staring at me as my entire body shook from adrenaline.

And then he'd told me to go. To leave and never look back. Because that was what he was going to do as well. I was just a memory to him. One that he was never going to think about again.

"Why did you stay?" slipped from my lips before I could stop the words.

His entire body stiffened. When he didn't say anything right away, I feared that I'd overstepped. "I—"

"I did leave."

My lips remained parted, but I forced my words back inside. If he was going to speak, I was going to let him.

"But I didn't get far before my granddad needed me to come back. And I've been here ever since." He reached down and picked up a rock. Then he tossed it into the water. It made a plunking sound, and the ripples on the surface spread out from where it had entered.

Silence engulfed the space between us. I wasn't sure if he was done or if he wanted me to say something, so I just stood there, staring out at the water. Suddenly, my line jerked, and the bobber sunk into the water. I gasped and quickly jerked the line to set the hook.

"Reel it in," Jax said as he stood, putting himself right next to me.

His sudden proximity threw me off guard for a moment, but luckily, I gathered my composure and focused on the task at hand before he realized my reaction.

I spun the handle as fast as I could, reeling the fish in, but then letting it out when the pole began to bend too far. Jax was cheering me on as I slowly brought it closer and closer until the fish was out of the water. Jax grabbed the line and pulled the fish onto the shore where he grabbed it.

"That's a nice-looking bass," he said as he began to work the hook out of its mouth. Its spotted skin glistened in the sun.

"That's a big one," I said, unable to keep myself from smiling. My heart was pumping with adrenaline, and I couldn't help but beam at the fish. It was silly, but I'd wanted so much to be a part of the fishing excursions my brothers used to go on. Catching a fish this big helped vindicate the little girl inside of me.

"Wanna release it or cook it?" Jax asked as he finished removing the hook and glanced up at me.

I studied it. As good as it felt to catch, I wasn't interested in eating it. I gave it a small smile. "Let him go. He can be a catch for someone else."

Jax glanced up at me as if to ask if I was sure. I gave him a nod, and he turned and slipped the fish back into the water and then rinsed his hands off and stood. "That was eventful," he said as he turned to face me, shaking the pond water off.

"That was," I said, loving the sense of satisfaction I felt.

He glanced over at me and just held my gaze for a moment. Then he sighed and shoved his hands into his front pockets. "I'm glad you caught something. It always helps turn my day around."

His smile made my stomach twist and turn. I hated and longed for it at the same time. I hated that he was being nice to me. He needed to hate me. So that I could hate me. If he liked me...if he kept looking at me like he was right now, I was going to hope.

And hope got me nowhere in life.

"I should go," I said as I set the fishing pole down and took a step back.

His eyebrows went up. "Oh, okay."

I paused before I nodded and turned, making my way

back up the bank. "I have to find Carmel. I'm sure she's around here somewhere." I tipped my face toward the east. "Carmel!" I yelled.

"I hope you find her," Jax said.

I hated the hopeful way those words were spoken. I hated that I could feel his gaze on me as I made my way back the direction I'd come. I hated that I wanted to turn around and thank him for helping me blow off some steam. For being there for me when I needed someone to talk to.

To thank him for not hating me like I hated myself.

Too scared of what I might say or do, I kept my gaze down as I made my way back toward the B&B. If that ridiculous dog wasn't there when I got back, I was going to get into my car and drive around looking for her. Apparently, walking around the grounds of my mother's house wasn't safe anymore. Not with Jax sneaking onto the property to fish.

I breathed a sigh of relief when the B&B's siding came into view. I broke through the trees and stepped out onto the lush green grass that my mother prided herself on maintaining.

My mouth dropped open when I saw Rose standing near the pool of water I'd been bathing Carmel in, rubbing that blasted dog down with her sudsy hands. I stomped over to them with my hands on my hips.

Rose turned to face me, her eyebrows raised. "What happened to you?"

I glowered at Carmel, who just looked up at me with her dark brown eyes.

"Traitor," I said.

"Were you looking long? Your cheeks are flushed." Rose leaned forward, inspecting my face.

I pulled back, not wanting her to push further. "I'm going to take a shower," I said as I started marching up the porch steps.

"What about Carmel?" Rose called after me.

"She looks perfectly content with you," I called over my shoulder.

I had no interest being outside right now with Rose and her million questions. I knew it was only a matter of time before she picked up on the fact that my flushed skin and pounding heart had nothing to do with the excursion to find Carmel and everything to do with Jax.

That was a truth I wanted to keep hidden for the rest of my life. Because if the truth came out, and I was forced to admit the thing that I'd buried a long, *long* time ago...there wasn't a way I could survive that.

My heart would break once more, and this time, it would never be able to come back together. And I'd be changed. Forever.

14

ABIGAIL

SWEET TEA & SOUTHERN GENTLEMAN

I moaned as I stretched out on the most comfortable bed I'd ever slept on. The sheets must have been made from the finest material because they felt like butter against my skin. And the mattress was fluffy, but not too much. My body sank into it, but it still managed to give enough structure that I didn't wake up sore.

In one night's sleep, I felt all of the stress that I'd built up over the last few months just slip away. I buried my face into the pillow and sighed.

This was not Harmony Island. This was not my home. And this was not my bed. I was in New York. With Bash.

What was I doing?

I flipped to my back and stared up at the vaulted ceiling. An ornate chandelier hung from the ceiling. What was this place? It had been so cold and quiet last night, I felt like I was sleeping in a museum. This couldn't have been Bash's childhood home.

What kind of childhood would that have been? Growing up in a house with more rooms than people. Large hallways that echoed your footsteps.

How did they even keep this place warm?

I remembered the small house I'd lived in with Mom and Dad. It was modest, just a two-story, four-bedroom house. Every time I smelled cinnamon, I was brought back to Christmas Eve when Mom would make a huge pot of cinnamon apple cider after her signature ham feast, and we would all sit around the table and sip the cider as we played card games.

Dad would build a fire in the living room, and the house would fill with warmth and laughter.

I closed my eyes as the dull ache that only came from losing a parent settled in my chest. I missed Mom so much sometimes that it hurt to breathe.

I opened my eyes, my thoughts turning back to Bash. Did he miss his mom? Did he miss his dad? Did he have Christmas memories like I did?

I dropped my arm over my eyes and sighed. Why was I thinking about this? Bash wasn't mine to worry about. I was here with Anders, and Bash left Harmony without even saying goodbye.

To think that he'd even missed me was foolish. I seemed to be the only one between the two of us who was thinking about the other person. I was foolish to entertain these thoughts.

I pulled off my covers and forced myself out of bed. When my feet hit the cool wood floor, I straightened and shuffled over to the bathroom, where I turned the shower on and slipped out of my nightgown. I closed my eyes once I was under the hot water and let my body relax.

The shampoo and conditioner that was stocked in the shower was a French brand. I couldn't read the labels, but it smelled like lavender and made my hair feel silky smooth when I was finished.

After I turned off the water, I grabbed one of the towels next to the shower and it felt like holding a cloud. I wasn't sure how I was ever going to go back to my life in Harmony after living in this kind of luxury.

How Bash had walked away from all this boggled my mind.

I dressed, brushed out my wet hair, and put on makeup while it air-dried. Then I took a blow-dryer to it before slipping on a pair of jeans and a white t-shirt.

My clothes felt basic compared to this house, and I hoped Bash wouldn't feel like I was disrespecting his father by dressing this way. Before I left the room, I stared at my reflection in the mirror. My heart began to race when, for a brief moment, my thoughts turned to Bash and what he would think when he saw me.

I shook my head, forcing those thoughts back into my mental lockbox, and headed to open my door.

The hallway was empty. I stopped at Anders' door, but when he didn't answer after my third knock, I shook my head, figuring that he was either sleeping or showering, and made my way down to the kitchen.

As I descended the stairs, I could hear some movement coming from the kitchen. I paused so I could gather the courage to enter. It had to be Bash, and I wasn't sure if I was quite ready to face him.

I felt ridiculous, standing at the bottom steps, steeling my nerves to face my boyfriend's best friend. I straightened, fisted my hands for strength, and headed into the kitchen.

My entire body froze when I saw Bash standing at the stove, shirtless, cracking an egg into a pan. My gaze drifted down his back and over the jagged pink lines that decorated his skin. I'd seen him shirtless before, back in Harmony in the apartment he shared with Anders, but I hadn't had the time to really take it all in.

I wondered where he got the scars from. Was it the accident he was in with his brother? It had to be. My thoughts flooded with questions, but I knew it wasn't my place to ask any of them. Even though I so desperately wanted to know. I wanted to figure out this man standing in front of me.

And then I realized that Bash had no idea I was standing here. He didn't know he was being watched. I felt like I was intruding on an intimate moment, so I quickly cleared my throat, which caused him to startle and whip his gaze over to me.

"Sorry," I said as I stepped fully into the room. Hopefully, he would assume that I'd just gotten here.

His gaze darkened before returning to the eggs. He looked on edge, his muscles tense, as he stared down at the pan. And then it hit me. He didn't want me here. He was probably incredibly annoyed that I'd come from Harmony. He was putting his dad to rest, not entertaining company.

Anders was his friend...I was not.

"I'm so sorry. I didn't mean to intrude," I said quickly as I turned to leave.

"Wait."

His voice caused my entire body to stop. I stared at the ground for a moment, waiting for him to continue.

The silence between us was deafening as the seconds ticked by. Was he controlling his frustration before he spoke? Was he picking his words carefully so as not to offend his best friend's girlfriend?

"Do you like sunny side up eggs?"

I glanced over my shoulder at him. He was facing me with a spatula in one hand and the pan of sizzling eggs in the other. I didn't want to leave, so I just nodded.

"Sure."

He held my gaze for a moment and then turned to set the pan down on the marble countertop. Then he rummaged around in the cupboard near the dishwasher and pulled out two plates.

I didn't know what he wanted me to do, so I just stood there watching as he set the plate down next to the pan.

"Eggs are something I don't let the chef prep for me. They're never good reheated the next day," he said as he slipped two of the eggs from the pan onto the first plate and then two onto the second plate. Then he nodded toward the loaf of bread sitting next to the fanciest toaster I'd ever seen. "Toast?"

"Sure."

He glanced at me for a moment before he undid the twist tie and pulled out a few slices to stick in the toaster. The clicking sound of the latch engaging filled the air, and I waited to see what Bash was going to do next.

He stood there, facing the toaster for a few seconds before he turned around. He folded his arms across his chest. His cheeks flushed as he glanced up at me. "Let me go get on a shirt."

He didn't wait for me to say anything. He crossed the kitchen and disappeared upstairs. With him gone, I felt a bit freer to move around the kitchen. After searching a few cupboards, I found a glass and filled it with the filtered water I found in the fridge. Just as I finished drinking, the toast popped up, so I pulled it out, thankful for a job to do.

I was spreading butter on the toast when Bash appeared once more, this time wearing a black t-shirt. My heart pounded as I glanced at him and then back at the toast, praying that he didn't notice me looking.

From the corner of my eye, I saw him study me. He lingered on the other side of the room, and his hesitation put me on edge. I felt like a nuisance, standing in the kitchen, finishing the toast. Had I overstepped? Was I making Bash feel uncomfortable in his own house?

"Sorry," I whispered as I stepped back, still holding the butter knife in my hand. "I thought I'd help out." I hesitated before I brought my gaze up to meet his.

His expression was unreadable. Electricity zapped between us. Time felt like it was standing still. I could feel my heart pounding in my ears, and I was acutely aware of each breath.

"Why are you here?" he finally asked. His expression was tortured as he stared at me, this time holding my gaze with an intensity that made me forget everything around me.

I parted my lips, but nothing came out. I just stood there, not sure how much time was passing. It was as if we were frozen in time. Neither of us knowing what to say, but not wanting to be the one who broke away first.

"I needed to thank you," I finally whispered.

His eyebrows drew together as he frowned. "I told you, consider me thanked."

"Do you want me to leave, then?" The words were out before I could stop them. I didn't want to leave. I wanted to be here. Around him. But if he didn't want me here, I would leave.

When he didn't speak right away, my heart began to pound once more. Did he want me here? Was it possible that he could want me like I was trying so desperately not to want him?

"It would be easier if you weren't here." His voice was so deep that I almost didn't hear him. He looked as if his words had pained him as he shoved his hands into the front pockets of his pajama pants.

Movement behind him drew my attention. Anders, fully dressed and hair damp, was coming down the stairs while scrolling on his phone. Not wanting to have him witness my very confusing interaction with Bash, I quickly turned and finished spreading butter on one of the pieces of toast.

Bash must have looked to see what had me returning to my task, because he suddenly appeared next to me as he opened the fridge and pulled out a jar of jam. "Strawberry jam?" he asked, setting it down next to me.

I proceeded to slather each slice with the jam as Bash and Anders filled the kitchen with conversation. Anders had so many questions about Bash's childhood.

Bash whipped up some eggs and toast for Anders, and soon we were all sitting down at the table, eating. Bash didn't look at me once while he chatted with Anders. It was like I wasn't even there. It was hard not to notice how at ease Bash was when he talked to Anders.

It was a stark difference from how he behaved when he spoke to me. He always seemed like he was in pain. As if being around me physically bothered him. I watched him laugh at something Anders said as I picked off pieces of my toast and slipped them into my mouth.

I narrowed my eyes, hating that he seemed to despise me so much, and yet, I couldn't seem to forget him. It didn't seem fair. Why couldn't I be as apathetic toward him as he seemed to be to me?

Their conversation turned serious when Anders asked him about his father. I was finished with my food, so I brought my plate to the sink. Even though I was intrigued, I didn't want Bash to feel uncomfortable with me there. After all, he seemed pretty determined to keep me at arm's length.

I turned on the faucet and let the water run hot before rinsing off my plate and grabbing the dish wand from the corner of the sink. The noise of the running water helped drown out their conversation. Even though I wanted to hear what Bash was saying, I knew my heart couldn't take it. It was better for me to remain in the dark then to try to open up to Bash and have my heart broken.

"I have a maid for that." Bash's voice startled me. My hand flew up—the one holding the dish wand—spraying the counter and Bash with sudsy water. He pulled back slightly as he blinked. Water droplets clung to his face. Realization of what I'd just done dawned on me, and I hurriedly dropped the dish wand and reached for a towel.

"I'm so sorry," I said as instinct took over and I began blotting his face with the towel.

"Abigail." Bash's voice was low and smooth.

My gaze drifted to his, and suddenly, I became very aware of just how close I was to him. And for some ridiculous reason, my gaze drifted down to his lips before I pulled it back up. If Bash noticed, he didn't step back. Instead, the warmth between our bodies grew to a burning heat, but neither of us moved to break the connection.

My hand remained frozen as it held the towel to Bash's face. My mind was screaming for me to step back. To drop my hand and laugh this whole situation off, but I couldn't. Instead, I just stood there, staring into Bash's eyes.

"Geez, Abby," Anders' voice broke the connection, and I was finally able to rip my gaze away from Bash. "Way to spray our host with gross sink water."

I dropped my hand and took a giant step back. But I couldn't move that far; I felt the cold marble countertop pressing into my back. "I'm so sorry," I said. My cheeks were on fire, and I was certain Bash and Anders could see my embarrassment.

A melodic ring had us all looking in the direction of the front door. Bash looked confused, but Anders perked up. He slapped Bash on the shoulder as he headed to the door.

"I ordered some toiletries to be delivered," he called over his shoulder as he disappeared down the hallway to the foyer.

I watched him until he disappeared. But once he was gone, I couldn't help but glance back at Bash. He hadn't moved from the sink. His gaze was conflicted, but for the first time since I'd gotten here, he didn't look as if he was about to sprint from the room.

"I'm sorry I sprayed you," I said, motioning toward his face.

He shook his head. "I shouldn't have startled you."

I hated the way his voice sounded. It sent shivers down my spine. It was low and smooth, and I could listen to it all day. I hated that he caused these reactions inside me. I needed him to tell me to leave. To tell me that he didn't feel this intensity between us that seemed to be clouding my judgement. That haunted my thoughts when I went to bed and was there to greet me as soon as I woke up in the morning.

I needed Bash to tell me that he wasn't interested so that I could finally be free of him. Or I was going to spend my life in love with a man that I could never have.

"Dude, you didn't tell me that you'd gotten engaged." Anders' voice drifted to my ears, but his words didn't register until I heard a female voice.

"Hey, Bash. I snuck in with the gardeners. I figured that you wouldn't mind."

A look passed across Bash's face as he glanced over at Anders. I did the same, and as soon as I saw her, my heart sank. She was perfection with her black jumpsuit, yellow high heels, and bright red hair pulled back into a tight bun at the nape of her neck.

She looked confused as she glanced between me and Bash. Her lips parted, and I could see the questions forming in her mind.

I hurried over to Anders and wrapped my arm around his waist. I leaned forward and met her gaze as I extended a hand. "My name is Abigail," I said. Thankfully, Anders didn't pick up on anything weird between me and Bash as he wrapped his arm around my shoulders.

"This is my girlfriend."

The woman closed her lips and nodded. "It's nice to meet the two of you." Then she glanced over at Bash. "Are they here for the funeral?" she asked as she crossed the room until she was standing next to Bash. Her heels clicked on the tile as she walked.

Bash nodded. "They came in from a small town in North Carolina."

Her arm slipped around Bash's waist while her other hand rested on his chest. "How sweet." Then she glanced up at him, her emerald green eyes putting the precious gem to shame. "Aren't you going to introduce?"

Bash glanced down at her. I could sense the hesitation in his gaze before he brought it back up to us. Then he sucked in his breath. "Guys, this is Emmeline. My fiancée."

15

CLAIRE

SWEET TEA & SOUTHERN GENTLEMAN

The sound of Carmel's barking broke through my dreams. I groaned as I reached out and patted around on my night-stand until I found my phone. It was way too early to be up.

"Carmel," I mumbled as I flipped to my back. I stared up at the time on the screen.

6:12

Ugh.

If I was woken up by the dog, that meant the guests at the B&B could also hear her. The last thing I needed was a negative review on Yelp that my mom would find. I was already taking a risk having a dog here on the property. If I was going to avoid my mother's wrath, I needed to keep the blasted dog a secret.

When Carmel's barking didn't relent, I pulled my covers off and stood. I threw my hair up into a messy bun, straightened my black tank over a pair of thrifted boxers, slipped my feet into my flip-flops, and headed out of my room.

Rose was already in the kitchen when I shuffled in. She gave me a pointed look. "That dog is barking again," she said as she uncovered the pan in front of her and the smell of garlic and eggs wafted up in the steam.

"I know, I know," I murmured as I wrapped my hand around the back door handle and yanked it open.

The grass was dewy, and the sun was just peeking up above the trees, painting the sky in purples and oranges. I hurried down the back porch steps and over to the shed that I'd set up for Carmel to live in.

Her tail was wagging, and she showered me with dog kisses when I stepped inside the dilapidated outbuilding. I'd watched my brothers build this place when we were kids, and it was barely hanging on after all of these years.

It seemed strange that my mother would keep such an eyesore on her property when she cared so much about presentation and order. It wasn't like she stored much for the B&B in here. There were just a few old pool things and some fishing gear that I remembered using as a kid.

"You have food. You have water." I reached down and rubbed Carmel's sides. "Why are you barking?" I crouched down in front of her, so she shoved her snout in my face and began kissing me again.

"Do you want to get out of here?" I asked as I stood and reached for the leash hanging by the door. As soon as she saw it, she started sprinting all around.

I laughed when I finally caught her between my legs so I could hook the clip to her collar. She kept her nose pressed to the crack of the door, and as soon as I started to open it, she began to wiggle her face through the opening.

It took a few minutes before she calmed down to a steady trot. I walked her down the gravel driveway toward the main road. The fresh summer-morning breeze washed over my skin, and I tipped my head back, welcoming its warmth.

The only thing that would make this more perfect were the sunglasses that I'd forgotten to grab on my way out.

I kept to the shoulder as we walked down the road that led into town. A few cars passed me, but it was still early, and Harmony was a small beach town. No one liked to be up before the sun could be seen. In the distance, the buildings were small. A sense of nostalgia pulled at my stomach as memories of growing up here flooded my mind.

I didn't hate this place. Sure, it was small and quirky, and everyone knew everyone else's business, but there was a sense of camaraderie that I hadn't been able to find anywhere else.

If my mother and I had a better relationship, I would consider staying longer. But whenever I was around her, I was reminded how much I disappointed her. And that was a life I couldn't live.

"On your left," a deep voice called.

Startled, I pulled on Carmel's leash and whipped around to see Jax on a bike behind me. He wore a helmet and workout clothes. When his gaze met mine, he slowed. My heart pounded in my chest.

"Claire? What are you doing out here?" he asked as he stopped his bike and slid off his seat. He caged the bike with his legs as he reached forward and grabbed the white water bottle that was clipped to one of the bars.

"Out for a morning walk," I said as I motioned to Carmel. I figured the dog on her leash would have given that away.

Jax didn't look at me. Instead, his gaze was trained on the tree line a few feet off. He whistled, and the branches of the bushes started to sway and wiggle until a chocolate lab burst out of the woods. He was panting around a giant stick in his mouth.

My hand wrapped around Carmel's leash as I pulled her closer, not knowing what this dog was going to do. But it seemed as if he only had eyes for Jax as he bounded over to him and dropped the stick at Jax's feet.

Jax reached out and rubbed the lab's neck before his fingers slipped around the dog's collar, which I was grateful for.

"You got a dog?" I asked.

He squinted up at me. "My sister got him for my nephew. I'm watching him for the weekend while they are gone to Disney."

I wouldn't have guessed that the dog wasn't his by the way he responded to Jax. But then again, a lot of people and animals were drawn to this man. It didn't surprise me that they already had an instant bond. It's why I fell so hard and so fast for Jax so many years ago.

Carmel was pulling at the leash to get closer to the lab. The lab in turn was straining against his collar as he tried to do the same.

Not wanting to chance a fight, since I really didn't know how Carmel would behave around another dog, I tightened the leash so she had to return to my side and started walking her a few feet back toward the B&B.

"It was good to see you, Claire," Jax called after me.

I just waved my hand in his direction as I kept my focus forward. I was certain I looked a mess in my bun and pajamas, which I was only now realizing I had left the house in.

I kept my pace quick. I wanted to get back to the B&B, take a shower, and pretend I was not bothered when Jax's gaze landed on mine.

How much easier would my life have been if I'd never known Jax? If I'd never kissed him? If I never allowed myself to love him?

"Idiot," I whispered under my breath as I rounded the B&B and made my way back to the shed. Once I got Carmel situated with water and food, I pushed a weight in front of the door in case she managed to unlatch it and hurried across the lawn and up the back porch steps.

I welcomed the blast of air-conditioned air that surrounded me as I stepped into the kitchen. Rose was nowhere to be seen. I could only guess that she was serving up breakfast in the dining room.

She'd filled two plates for us and set them on the table, so I made my way over and sat down. After a long drink of water, I scooped up some eggs and slipped them into my mouth. My eyes instantly closed as I let out a slow moan. These were heaven.

"You're an angel," I said to Rose as she pushed through the swinging door and stepped into the kitchen.

She chuckled as she set a serving platter down on the counter and hurried over. I could feel her gaze rake over me as she slowly lowered herself onto a chair. I braced myself for the questions I knew were coming.

"Why are your cheeks so flushed?" she asked as she picked up her mug of coffee that had swirls of steam rising off it and gingerly took a sip.

"I was walking Carmel," I said through the eggs I was chewing.

"This is a different kind of pink. It's a pink reserved only for a certain someone."

I groaned as I grabbed the nearby cloth napkin and covered my face with it.

"I knew it," she cheered next to me.

"I was walking Carmel, and he just...showed up." He seemed to be doing that a lot since I got back. Invading my space when I least expected it.

Rose was quiet, so I peeked over the napkin at her. She was eyeing me with a satisfied smile on her lips as she methodically took a bite from the toast she was holding in her hand.

"You know, I never believe in coincidences. Everything happens for a reason." She took another bite and grinned at me.

I glared at her as I shoveled the rest of my food into my mouth. The last thing I needed was to sit here and listen to her talk about how Jax and I were somehow destined to be together.

With my plate now empty, I grabbed my dishes and set them in the sink. My mouth was still full as I made my way toward the hallway that led to my room.

"There's no such thing as a coincidence," Rose sung out after me.

I mumbled something incoherent as I disappeared into my room and shut the door. Now alone, I closed my eyes and leaned against the wall. My heart was pounding, and I hated that I still reacted this way to conversations about Jax.

I needed to be stronger. I only needed to survive until Mom was back and I was certain that she and Rose could handle things. Then I was going to leave and never come back.

And Jax would go right back to where he'd been all the years that I'd been gone. In the lockbox in my mind that I never opened.

16

BASH

There were two times in my life that I remembered as being moments that turned my life upside down. The first was when I woke up in the hospital after the accident and my father informed me that Carson was gone. I remembered the pain as acutely now as when I heard those words amongst the beeping of my monitors.

The second time was right now. Standing in the kitchen with Emmeline's arm wrapped tightly around me as the words I just uttered lingered in the air. I would never forget the look on Abigail's face after my confession. She was trying to hide it, but it impacted her, and that broke my heart even more than it already was.

I'd wanted so desperately not to hurt her. That's why I left. That's why I kept my distance from her even though that was akin to torture. I never let myself feel freely the things I wanted to feel for her. And I worked so hard to keep her from feeling those things for me.

But now, seeing all of the color drain from her face as she shifted her gaze from me to Emmeline and then to the floor, a sense of dread filled my chest and exploded throughout my body. She couldn't be feeling for me what I felt for her...could she?

The only person allowed to hurt in this world was me because it's what I deserved. Happiness is for good people. And nothing I could ever do would redeem me from killing my brother.

"That's great!" Anders said, drawing my attention over to him. He let go of Abigail and crossed the room to give me a handshake turned hug.

I went through the motions, clapping him on the back. My gaze went to Abigail, who seemed to be staring off into space before slowly glancing over at me. She brought up one hand across her stomach so she could grasp her opposite elbow and forced a smile.

I wished in that moment I could say something that would make her feel better, but nothing currently occupying my mind seemed appropriate. So I just nodded and pulled back when Anders released me from the hug. He turned his attention to Emmeline and gave her a handshake before pulling her into a hug. I stood awkwardly to the side, not sure what to do.

"Congrats." Abigail's voice neared, and it sent shivers across my skin.

When I glanced down at her, she was looking up at me. In that moment, I would have given up all of my father's wealth to know what she was thinking.

Did she hate me?

I wished she would. If she hated me, living a life without her would be manageable. Her hatred would fuel my survival. But her love? That would kill me right here where I stood.

She lifted her arms, and I knew at that moment she would give me a hug. I wanted to run from the room and never look back. I feared that if I touched her again, the memory of her body against mine would haunt me for the rest of my life.

But if that was what she wanted, I wasn't going to be the one to deny her. I slowly wrapped my arms around her waist and drew her to me. She made a small gasp next to my ear, like I was squeezing the breath from her when I bent closer, closing the space between us. Her arms wrapped fully around my neck and her body pressed to my chest. I wondered if she could feel my pounding heart.

It was a dead giveaway for what I felt for her.

"I mean it. I'm happy that you've found happiness," she said as she began to pull away.

I wanted to draw her back to me and never let go, but that would be inappropriate and confusing. I couldn't do that to her. So I fought against my desire to keep her close as I watched her pull back and shift her attention to Emmeline.

Their hug was quick, and when they were finished,

Emmeline shifted her attention back over to me, slipping her arm around my waist once more. I really wished she would stop doing that, but she was to be my wife. I needed to be okay with physical attention from her.

"So, what's the plan for today?" Emmeline asked as she wrapped both arms around me and peered up at me.

I glanced over at Abigail, who was leaning against Anders, who was using the edge of the counter as support. When Emmeline moved as if she were trying to get my attention, I dropped my gaze to her.

"We should be getting Dad's ashes by this afternoon. The funeral home expedited his cremation. There's a memorial of sorts, and then Dad wants his remains scattered in the ocean. So tonight, we'll be getting on his yacht and setting sail."

Emmeline sighed. "I get seasick." She pulled back. "I'm really sorry. I get, like, puke over the side of the railing the whole time sick. But I can make it to the memorial."

I glanced down at her. Her eyes were wide, and her bottom lip was poking out as if she thought pouting would make up for the fact that she wouldn't be there when I spread my father's ashes. Truth was, I didn't have strong feelings about her coming or staying. I guess I just preferred her to be honest with me instead of trying to garner sympathy with puppy-dog eyes.

"That's fine," I said, giving her a nod. It's not like she knew my dad other than through a bad business deal. I couldn't really blame her for not wanting to go.

"Well, we can be there." Anders clapped me on the shoulder once more. "Just tell us when and where."

———

MY SUIT once again felt as if it were strangling me. I adjusted my tie in front of the mirror as I stared at my reflection, hating everything I saw there. My hair was slicked back, revealing the jagged scar on my face. I'd grown accustomed to showing it ever since I got back.

Before, I'd used my hair to hide my face, fearing that people would recognize me. But now, everyone knew who I was. And the few times Dad had been awake enough to know who I was, he'd glared at my appearance like it offended him, so I'd made a point to clean up.

Now, I couldn't bring myself to relax. I wasn't sure who I was anymore. I was living the life everyone else expected me to live. I'd lost myself the day Carson died, and nothing could bring that person back.

Well, nothing *I* could do. But there was a person who made me feel alive again. She was currently sharing a wall with me and invading my thoughts in a way I didn't deserve.

"Idiot," I whispered as I slammed the light switch off, and I headed out of the bathroom.

I was engaged to Emmeline. *Engaged.* I wasn't free anymore. I needed to stop thinking about Abigail and move on.

I pulled open my door and stopped in my tracks when I

was met with Abigail's wide eyes as she stared up at me. I glanced down to see that her hand was raised like she was about to knock.

"I—um..." She closed her beautiful, perfect lips and swallowed.

I watched her as she tried to gather her thoughts. But before she could speak, my entire body went into flight mode, and all I could think about in that moment was kissing her. I'd held back for so long. I felt so broken. All I wanted was to feel something.

My hands found her waist, and I pulled her into my room and pressed her against the wall next to the door. My body covered hers as I leaned in, begging her to let me kiss her.

Her eyes were wide as she stared up at me, but she didn't look panicked. Instead, her gaze turned hazy as her hands slowly slid from my chest up to the back of my neck.

That was all I needed. For this one moment in time, she was going to be mine. And I wasn't going to waste a moment of it.

My lips found hers like she was a lighthouse in the ocean and I was a ship lost at sea. My heart pounded in my chest as I closed my eyes, memorizing the feel of her body, her lips, and her hands as they moved over me.

I caged her in with my arms, fearing that if I didn't, she would somehow float away.

She deepened the kiss, and I moaned as my willpower slowly slipped away. My hands left their post as I wrapped my arms around her waist so I could hoist her further up the wall and kiss her more fully.

And then reality hit. It crashed into me so hard, that all I could do was drop her to her feet and pull my entire body back until I slammed into the wall on the other side of the room.

I was an idiot. I was such a freaking idiot. I'd just kissed my best friend's girl. I was engaged. What the hell did I just do?

"I'm so sorry," I whispered as I kept my focus trained on the ground in front of me. I couldn't bring myself to look at her. I'd messed up. I was *always* messing up.

"It's okay," she said.

The cadence of her voice made me close my eyes. She was so pure. So *good*. And I was everything bad. I didn't deserve to want her. I didn't deserve to kiss her. To hold her in my arms and make love to her.

I'd broken my promise, and I was never going to forgive myself for doing that.

"Bash." The feeling of her hand on my arm shocked me into opening my eyes.

I looked down to see her staring up at me. The skin around her mouth was red, and her lips looked swollen. But her gaze, her forgiving gaze, just made me feel worse.

"It's okay. Don't beat yourself up about this. It was just a kiss."

Just a kiss. Those words felt like daggers to my heart, but at the same time, they gave me hope. It was just a kiss for her. To me, it was my lifeblood. But to her, it was just two people getting lost in the moment.

"Grief makes you do silly things," she said as she dropped her hand and took a step back. "No one can fault you for that." She cleared her throat. "I'm sure if Emmeline had been the one at your door, you would have kissed her like that." Her smile was small as she studied me.

Didn't she know? She had to know how I felt about her. That she was my world. When she was around, I could feel the earth under my feet. I felt...alive. And when she was gone, I was a shell. Moving from place to place, living my life for whoever wanted to control it at that moment.

"I'm sorry," I repeated. There were so many things I wanted to say, but I couldn't say any of them.

She pinched her lips together and nodded. "I know. And I forgive you." She sighed. The sound was melodic and sweet. "I kissed you back, so it wasn't all your fault." Her cheeks flushed as she said those words.

I stared at her, hoping she could see how I felt. But she didn't linger. Instead, she glanced over at me before turning her attention back to the hallway and took a few steps through the doorway until she was standing outside once more.

"What I came to say was, Anders and I are ready and waiting downstairs." She brushed down the front of her dress, and for the first time since opening the door, I took in her entire appearance.

She was wearing a black dress that was covered in lace.

Her hair fell around her shoulders in soft ringlets. She looked beautiful, and my mouth twitched to tell her that, but I'd already messed up. There was no reason to do it again.

I just nodded, grabbed my bedroom door handle, and headed out into the hallway after her. We walked in silence as we made our way down the stairs and toward the voices that could be heard in the living room.

Emmeline was standing near the bookshelf, and Anders was next to her with a tumbler full of amber liquid in his hand. My stomach lurched at the sight of him drinking, but I didn't say anything. After all, a few drinks didn't do much to alter Anders. It was Anders after ten drinks that made the hair on the back of my neck stand up.

"Are you drinking?" Abigail's voice was hushed.

I hated that the slightest hint of worry from her spiked my protective mode. I glanced over to see her studying Anders. Her lips were tight, and her eyebrows were drawn together as she studied him.

Anders looked sheepish. He sauntered over to her and draped his arm around her shoulders. "It's just a drink, love. One won't hurt me."

Abigail wasn't happy with his response. Her expression didn't change, and she stiffened when he dropped the weight of his arm onto her. But there was nothing I could do to get him off. He was the one she was dating, not me. I would do well to remember that.

"Are you ready to go?" Emmeline appeared next to me, her gaze soft as she smiled.

Guilt coated my insides as I nodded, and she slipped her arm through mine. I knew I needed to come clean to her. After all, I'd been the one to initiate the kiss. She deserved to know. But right at this moment, it didn't feel appropriate. After all, we were headed to my father's memorial service.

I would tell her tomorrow. Once Abigail and Anders were gone, and whatever my future life held for me had started.

In the limo, Nicholas sat up front next to the driver as we headed to the funeral home. Anders and Abigail sat on one side while Emmeline and I sat on the other. Abigail was directly in front of me, our feet occasionally touching when the limo took a tight turn. I didn't allow myself to look directly at her, and she seemed to be doing the same.

When we arrived, I blew out my breath, ready to get out of these close quarters. I waited for everyone to exit before I climbed out last. There was a crowd of paparazzi standing on the other side of the ropes that had been put up to keep the guests safe.

I kept my head down as I buttoned my suit coat and followed the other three up the steps to the entrance. Once inside, the funeral director saw me and hurried over.

He handed me a program before looking up at me and asking, "Are you ready for this?"

I swallowed against the lump of regret that had formed in my throat, making it impossible to breathe, and said, "As ready as I'll ever be."

17

ABIGAIL

SWEET TEA &
SOUTHERN GENTLEMAN

I was going to Hades.

A person who is at a funeral but is only thinking about the illicit kiss they shared with the deceased's son is destined to go there.

Did Bash shock me when he pulled me into his room and kissed me like no man had ever kissed me before? Yes.

Should I forget that kiss and never think about it again? Absolutely.

Was I actually going to be able to keep the memory at bay for the rest of my life? Nope.

I was doomed.

My gaze drifted over to Bash. I was sitting behind and to the left of him. I could see his profile. His jaw muscles twitched as he stared up at the man conducting the service. He was tense, his shoulders drawn taut, and his hands sprawled out on his thighs. I sighed, wanting to help him relax but knowing that wasn't my place.

That was his fiancée's job. The woman who was sitting next to him. Whose arm and thigh were brushing his.

This was torture.

"You okay?" Anders' whisper snapped my attention away from Bash.

I glanced over at him, the faint smell of alcohol on his breath made my stomach twist. I hated that he'd taken a drink. It felt like the new Anders was gone and the old Anders was back.

"What do you mean?" I asked, pushing away my frustration when I saw he looked genuinely concerned.

"You're glaring at Bash."

I instantly relaxed my face, squinting my eyes a few times. "I think I'm just tired."

I saw Anders nod from the corner of my eye before blowing out his breath. "Me too."

I spent the rest of the service keeping my gaze away from Bash. I only allowed myself to look at him when he went up to the microphone to recall a few memories about his dad. He looked panicked and forlorn when the only stories he could come up with were ones from his childhood.

My heart broke when his voice turned to a whisper, and then he grabbed a tissue, excused himself, and sat back down. I wished I could reach out and offer him a sympathetic shoulder squeeze, but that would only confuse me more.

Anders didn't miss a beat and reached forward to pat his shoulder a few times. Bash turned back to give him a thankful nod, and as he did, his gaze caught mine. My smile was pathetic, but thankfully, his gaze didn't linger long.

The funeral director got up after the pastor finished and informed us that there were refreshments in the back. We waited for Bash to stand. He was followed by a woman, who I could only assume was his sister-in-law, and a little boy. Once they were gone, the rest of us stood and followed them.

Anders and I stayed on the outskirts of the room where the refreshments were being served. He downed a few flutes of champagne. I watched him warily. I didn't like him drinking, and I thought we'd been on the same page about it.

Apparently not.

When he took another flute as a waiter passed him, I excused myself and headed to the hors d'oeuvres table. I found a small plate and stepped into line. I was dishing up a few crackers with some kind of mousse topped with caviar, when suddenly I was shoved forward. Before I could stop myself, I landed on top of the trays in front of me, smashing the food into my dress.

"Timothy!"

I scrambled to extricate myself from the mess, and when I glanced down at myself, I cringed. I was covered in fancy food.

"I'm so sorry." A woman's voice sounded next to me. When I glanced over, I saw Bash's sister-in-law zeroing in on me with a wad of napkins in her hands. "I don't know what's gotten into that boy."

"It's okay," I stammered, still completely out of sorts from what had just happened.

The sister-in-law was wiping my dress with the napkins, but it wasn't doing much to the mousse. She sighed and looked up at me. "Come with me to the bathroom. I think some water will help."

"Are you okay?" Bash's voice made my heart pound. He must have run over to us. The last time I'd checked on him, he was on the other side of the ballroom.

"She's fine," Emery said as she grabbed my hand and started pulling me after her. "Watch Timothy for me," she called over her shoulder to a woman with a jet-black bob. The woman nodded and headed after the little boy.

When we got to the bathroom, she led me over to the sink. She turned the hot water on and leaned over to grab some paper towels.

"I really don't know what's got into him," she repeated as she wetted the towels and turned to me.

"It's fine. Really. I wasn't a big fan of this dress to begin with." I tried to catch her gaze, but she seemed focused on cleaning me up.

"You're kind to say that," she said as she reached forward and began to dab the dress. "When you get home, send me the bill for the dry cleaning, and I'll get it taken care of."

"I'll probably just throw it away," I joked, trying to lighten the mood.

Her expression turned mortified, so I reached down and grabbed her hands, hoping she would look at me. That seemed to do the trick because she stopped moving and slowly brought her gaze up to meet mine.

"Really, it's fine." I gave her a soft smile. "You're dealing with a lot. The last thing you need to worry about is this ten-year-old dress."

She studied me, and then slowly she began to relax until she slumped against the counter. She buried her face in her hands, and shortly after, I could hear soft sobs coming from behind them.

I shifted until I was next to her and hesitated before I wrapped an arm around her shoulders and let her cry. I understood how she felt even though I didn't understand her pain. Her cries were the cries of a broken heart.

"I'm so sorry," I whispered.

We just stayed there in silence. Me with my arm wrapped around her shoulders, staring down at the floor. Emery with her face buried in her hands, her shoulders moving up and down as she cried.

Eventually, her tears subsided, and she straightened. I removed my arm, giving her some space. She kept her hands pressed to her cheeks as she took in a deep breath with her eyes closed. I reached over to grab a box of tissues and handed them to her.

She pulled out a few and dabbed underneath her eyes

before turning to face the mirror. "I'm so sorry. I don't know what that was about."

"You just lost your father-in-law."

Emery glanced up at me in the mirror. "Do I know you?"

I shook my head. I hoped she didn't think that I was some creepy stalker. And I wasn't sure who I was to Bash, so I went with the most simplistic answer. "My boyfriend is friends with Bash."

She paused, her hand frozen on her cheek. "So, you know Bash?"

Know him? I'd just shared a mind-blowing kiss with him a few hours ago. My cheeks heated at the memory, and I knew if I kept thinking about it, the words were going to eventually slip out. I needed to keep everything pertaining to Bash out of my mind.

"Kind of." There. Simple and hopefully didn't invite a lot of questions.

She glanced down at the ground while she folded and unfolded the tissue a few times. "Do you ever have regrets?"

"Regrets?"

She didn't look up. Instead, she just nodded before she closed her eyes. "I have regrets. A lot of them."

I had a lot of regrets as well. "I think regrets come with being human. You make choices in the moment, but only time will tell if those choices were right or wrong." I rubbed my forehead as I felt a tension headache coming on. "What's the saying? Hindsight is twenty-twenty?"

She chuckled. "Yeah...Has Bash said anything about me?" Her voice was a whisper now.

"No. He hasn't said anything about you." Her question piqued my interest, and I wanted to ask more questions, but I didn't want to pry.

She glanced over at me. "Nothing?"

I frowned. "What would he say about you?"

She sighed and glanced back down at the tissue in her hands. "I figured he hated me and blasted me to all his friends."

"That doesn't sound like Bash."

She paused and then shrugged. "I don't really know him anymore. Ever since Carson..." Her voice broke, so she closed her lips as tears welled up in her eyes. My heart broke for her, and I reached out and wrapped my arm around her once more. She nodded, and when she took a deep breath, I dropped my arm so she wouldn't feel like I was smothering her.

"Things just changed. And they've never gone back."

I nodded. I'd never lost a spouse, but I'd lost my mom. Nothing could ever be the same after that. I didn't want to take away from her experience, so I just whispered, "I'm so sorry."

She closed her eyes for a moment. "Thank you."

We stood there in silence. Memories of my broken relationship with Dad raced through my mind. It was as if I were meant to be here, standing in this bathroom with

Emery. I was going to regret not saying something if I didn't speak up now.

"Have you talked to him about this?" I asked.

She glanced over at me, her eyes puffy and red, but the tears had subsided. "Talked to who?"

"Bash?"

Her eyes widened before she shook her head. "He doesn't want to talk to me."

I frowned. That didn't sound like Bash. Regardless of how he'd handled life after his brother's death, the man I knew wanted nothing more than to take care of the people in his life.

"I don't think that's true. I'm sure he's just waiting for you to reach out."

She scoffed and shook her head. "He hates me. He hates his father. He stayed away for so long, I don't even know who that man is anymore." She wiped her nose with her tissue.

"I thought that, too," I whispered as I folded my arms across my chest and leaned against the counter. "I didn't think Bash cared about me at all. But the night my sister and nephew went missing..." My entire chest squeezed around my heart, making it impossible to breathe.

She looked over at me.

I closed my eyes as the memory of my empty apartment and not knowing where Sabrina and Samuel were came flooding back to me. I took a deep breath to steel my nerves. "He went out after them. He found them and brought them back." I glanced over at her once more. "I think no matter how hard you push Bash, he'll never truly leave you. I think all he wants is for you to be happy. And he thinks that the only way to accomplish that is by staying away."

Her expression stilled as she watched me. I could see her processing my words. Then she sniffled again and nodded. "You're a good friend to Bash. I'm glad he found people who care about him."

"Thanks." The word *friend* echoed in my mind, but I pushed the aching feeling away as I smiled. "And he has Emmeline to take care of him once we're gone."

Her body tensed at the mention of Bash's fiancée. Her gaze dropped to the floor before she shifted it to the tissue box and pulled another one out. "Emmeline," she whispered.

Her reaction and the way she said Emmeline's name piqued my curiosity. I glanced over at her and waited to hear more.

"They just met." She sighed, blew her nose, and grabbed another tissue before searching for the garbage to toss the used one.

"What do you mean they just met?"

"His dad and Emmeline's dad came up with an agreement to save Torres Investments from a deal that went bad with Deveraux Construction."

"An agreement?"

Emery nodded. "A marriage."

I stared at her. She had to be joking. "I thought something like that only happened in novels or the movies."

She shrugged. "I guess they were old-school when it came to this plan."

For some reason, my heart felt lighter. Bash didn't love Emmeline. He was being forced into the marriage. Did that mean he could...care about me like I cared about him?

That kiss had me thinking so.

And then my mind settled on something I hadn't picked up on earlier. "Did you say Deveraux Construction?"

She glanced over at me and nodded. "Yeah, why?"

"Deveraux Construction? Like, the company trying to buy out Harmony Island?"

She stared at me. "How did you know about that?"

I swallowed, my head spinning. "That's where I'm from. That's where my business is." Bash knew? Why didn't he say something?

"What a small world."

I didn't know what to say. I'd gone into this bathroom with Emery thinking we were just going to make small talk as I cleaned up my dress. Now, I felt more confused than when I got in here. I had so many questions for Bash, but I wasn't sure if I even had the right to ask them.

Emery blew out her breath, dumped the tissues into the garbage, and then turned to offer me a small smile. "Thanks for talking to me. You probably don't realize it, but you helped me feel a lot better."

I smiled and nodded. "I'm glad I could help." I just wished I could say the same.

"I'm serious about the dry-cleaning bill. Send it to me, and I'll take care of it." She nodded toward my dress that had crusty mousse still stuck on it.

I waved her words away and watched as she opened the bathroom door and headed out. I glanced into the mirror, staring at my reflection for a moment. If Bash wasn't marrying Emmeline because he loved her, did it mean that he might...love me?

My heart pounded at the thought. The memory of his hands on my body and his lips pressed to mine rushed through my mind. I wanted it to be real. But I couldn't allow myself to hope that. Not when he'd committed himself to Emmeline. There was no way I could ask him to break that off. He wanted to save his father's company, and he seemed determined to do just that.

I pulled my focus from my reflection and grabbed some paper towels and stuck them under the water. Then I started to blot at the food that had formed a crust amongst the lace.

"Are you okay?"

My entire body froze as Bash's smooth voice filled the room. My heart ached as I realized that, very soon, I was going to have to walk away from him, never to see him again.

"I'm fine," I whispered as I kept my focus on my dress.

I could feel his presence as he walked closer to me. His shadow soon surrounded me. "I'm sorry for my nephew."

Tears brimmed my eyes, but I wasn't going to let him see me cry. I just shook my head. "It's fine. Kids can be clumsy."

"I sent Nicholas home to get you a change of clothes. He should be back really soon."

I hated that he was being nice to me. I hated that I knew he didn't love Emmeline. And I hated that every time he spoke, I wanted him to admit his feelings to me so I could stop living in this torture. "Thanks. That'll help."

Bash fell quiet, but I could feel his gaze on me. His desire to speak felt as palpable as the humidity in Harmony during the hot summer months. I waited, my ears perked to take in whatever he wanted to say.

But no words came. Instead, his phone chimed, and he mumbled that Nicholas had returned.

I sighed as soon as the door thudded behind him. I leaned against the wall and tipped my head up and closed my eyes.

No matter how I felt, Bash was taken. And even if I wanted to believe that he cared for me, it didn't matter. He was marrying Emmeline, and there was nothing I could do to stop him.

With the way I was feeling, I knew I was in love with him. I wanted to be the woman he kissed at night and cooked breakfast for in the morning. I wanted to be the woman he made love to and the one to bear his children.

Being around him was breaking my heart, so I needed to leave. I needed to break things off with Anders and return to Harmony to hide out until I could breathe again.

I needed to say goodbye to Bash and never look back. Or I was going to crumble and never be able to put myself back together again. And I couldn't have that happen.

I needed to be there for Dad and Sabrina. Right now, they were going to be my focus. Not Bash. Not Emmeline.

And not my broken and smashed-to-smithereens heart.

18

BASH

SWEET TEA &
SOUTHERN GENTLEMAN

The memorial service only lasted for a half hour more before I told Nicholas I was done and to ask everyone to leave. He was quick at clearing a room, and soon, it was just me, Emmeline, Anders, and Abigail who remained.

Emmeline had her arm wrapped around mine as we stood in the middle of the room as the waiters and waitresses began to clear the tables and chairs.

My gaze kept drifting over to Abigail who was trying to talk to a very intoxicated Anders. My fingers curled into a fist as I watched him stumble a bit when Abigail tried to direct him to the nearest chair.

When he tripped and his hands flung out to catch his balance, the only thing he grabbed was Abigail's midsection. I pulled away from Emmeline and headed in their direction. I wasn't going to stand by and watch as he grabbed at Abigail.

"Come on," I said as I grabbed his arm and draped it over my shoulders. Then I wrapped my other arm around his midsection and pulled him against my side for support.

In a few quick steps, I led him over to a chair and set him down on it.

I didn't need this. I was confused and hurting already. I didn't need to hate my friend because he couldn't handle his alcohol.

"I'm so sss-orry man," he slurred as he glanced up at me, his eyes glassy.

I couldn't hate the man. After all, I'd been him not so long ago. Maybe that's why I kept our relationship going. If I could help him, that would somehow make up for the things I'd done when I was like him.

"It's okay," I said as I reached down and clapped him on the shoulder.

His body shook from the movement, so I dropped my hand. Abigail was standing next to me and was chewing on her thumbnail as she stared at Anders.

"Nicholas will take him home. He'll be fine," I said, my voice low.

She looked up at me. There was something in her gaze. A look that had my heart pounding. Something had changed between me and her. I wanted to believe that it had something to do with our kiss, but I quickly squashed those thoughts as they just confused me.

"Okay," she whispered.

I gave her a quick smile and then turned to move away from her. To get to a place where I felt like I could breathe.

"Anders isn't going with you on the boat?" Emmeline asked as she neared me, making my hasty retreat impossible.

I glanced back at my friend and shook my head. "He's going home."

"So, you're going to be alone?" Her eyes were wide.

There was no way I was going to ask Abigail to go with me, and Emmeline had already made it clear that she wasn't able to go.

"I'll be fine," I said, holding her gaze and hoping that she would believe me.

She shook her head as her gaze drifted over to Abigail. "Why don't you go with him?" she asked.

Abigail's eyes widened. "Me?"

Emmeline nodded.

Anders grabbed Abigail's hand. "You can't leave Bash to do this alone. Go with him," he mumbled.

Abigail slowly brought her gaze up to meet mine. Then she shrugged. "If you want me to go, I can."

I wanted her to go. My heart was pounding, and my soul was singing at the thought of her coming with me. But I was an idiot if I thought this offer had anything to do with her feelings for me. She needed to be convinced to go. I would do well to remember that. "If you want to come, it's fine."

Our gazes locked and I could see the trepidation in her eyes before she nodded. "I'll come."

"Great," Emmeline sung out.

Nicholas joined us, and I helped him half hold, half carry Anders from the room. Once he was situated in the limo, I shut the door, and Nicholas told the driver where to take him.

Emmeline was walking up behind me when I turned around as the limo drove away. She gave me a smile before reaching up onto her tiptoes and pressing her lips to my cheek.

"I hope you can forgive me for not going with you," she said as she pulled back. Her expression had turned sheepish.

I had a lot to confess to her, but right here, with Nicholas and the valet on either side of me, didn't seem like the right place to do it. I just nodded. "Of course."

A red car drove up, and a valet got out. Emmeline smiled as she lifted her hand in a quick wave and walked toward the open driver's door. The valet handed her the keys, and I watched as she situated herself in the car and then pulled out into traffic. Now alone, I glanced back to the building to see Abigail standing near the door looking as if she wasn't sure what she was supposed to do.

My heart pounded as I met her gaze, and then I dropped it and walked toward her. "Come on," I whispered as I passed her.

She didn't respond, and I didn't stop to see if she was following me. I just kept walking, praying that I would survive the rest of the night.

THE WARM, salty air whipped around me as Nicholas steered the boat through the waves. The ocean was awake tonight, and the normally calm water had our boat jumping and tilting. Abigail was sitting on one of the leather seats inside, but I was too antsy, so I stayed outside, leaning on the railing and watching the ocean move underneath me.

We didn't really speak during the car ride to the dock. Which I was okay with. I wasn't sure what I would say if I allowed myself to speak. I feared what I would confess, and I didn't need the added confusion that I was already feeling from the kiss we shared.

Keeping my distance from her seemed to be the best plan of action.

I really wasn't sure where I was supposed to spread Dad's ashes. "In the ocean" was all the instruction he gave us. I told Nicholas to just drive and I'd let him know when I was ready to get this done.

I tipped my head forward and closed my eyes, taking in a deep breath of ocean air. I had very few good memories of being out here with Dad. Most times, when we did go out, he would spend his time inside on the phone, and Carson and I would play on the deck with our nanny.

But for some reason, even those memories were short and uneventful. I would have given anything to go back to that time.

The feeling of something heavy dropping on my shoulders had me straightening and glancing over. Abigail froze, her gaze meeting mine. I could see from the corner of my eye that her arms were raised as if she'd just set something on me.

My hands rose up, and the soft warmth of a cashmere blanket brushed my fingertips.

"I thought you might be cold," she said.

As soon as we got on the boat, I'd slipped off my suit coat, removed my tie, and rolled up the sleeves of my button-down shirt. I'd kicked off my shoes and was walking around in my dress socks.

Nicholas had found a pair of slacks and a white lace shirt for Abigail to change into, and I hated every part of it. She'd looked beautiful before, but now she looked like an angel, standing in front of me with her wide eyes and caring look.

It made every part of my body ache for her touch.

"You're not being fair," I mumbled under my breath.

I didn't expect her to hear, but when she leaned forward, I realized she'd picked up on some of my words.

"What?" she asked.

I sighed and pushed my hand through my hair as I leaned forward on the railing in front of me. "Nothing."

She didn't respond. Instead, she just remained still as she kept her post next to me. I wanted her to go. I wanted to command her to leave. I wasn't sure I had the strength to stay away from her if she remained.

"Tell me something about your dad," she said. Her voice was low, and it sent shivers down my spine.

"My dad?" I asked, glancing over at her.

Her hands were on the railing next to me. She was facing the ocean now; her gaze was trained on the dark water below. "You dad. Your mom...Carson."

I clenched my jaw at the mention of my brother's name. But then I blew out my breath. If I was going to return to this world, I needed to be okay with talking about the man I'd tried to forget when I left.

"You've never told me about your mom."

I fiddled with the edge of the blanket. "She died from cancer when I was young."

"I'm sorry."

I peeked over at her. "Thanks."

"That had to be hard, growing up without a mom."

I nodded. "Especially when you have a distant dad."

She met my gaze. "You have no good memories of your father?"

I scoffed. If only she'd met the man, then she would understand. "My father was not a nurturing type." Then I stopped. There was one memory. Though there were times when I wondered if I'd just dreamed it.

"There was one time," I whispered, my emotions taking hold of my throat and choking me.

Abigail didn't speak, so I continued.

"I was young. Six or seven. Dad took us out onto the boat." I patted the railing with my hand. "Not this one, a smaller one. We went out at dusk, and Dad just drove around. Mom was wrapped in a white linen blanket, and she kept smiling and laughing at whatever he was saying."

Tears pricked my eyes, and I wanted to stop, but the words just kept flowing. "Carson and I laid out watching the stars. He fell asleep, but I couldn't. Then I heard soft music playing, and when I snuck to the back, I found Mom and Dad dancing. She was tucked against his chest, and he was just holding her and swaying to the music."

I cleared my throat, hoping to dislodge the painful ache in my chest but failing miserably at it. Why did everyone have to be gone? Didn't they realize what they were doing when they all left me here? Alone.

A warm hand enveloped mine. I glanced down to see that Abigail was touching me. My heart began to pound. I wanted so much more than what I could have. I was so desperately in love with this woman that I was physically incapable of staying away from her.

But she could never be mine. And I wasn't going to do that to her.

I slipped my hand out from under hers and pushed it through my hair. I cleared my throat as I stared out into the dark abyss that was the ocean in front of me. I swallowed, unable to meet her gaze, and headed toward the enclosed cabin. "I'm going to get Dad's ashes," I muttered under my breath.

I didn't wait to see if she was going to follow me. Instead, I pulled open the door and stepped into the elegant cabin that my father had designed himself. I walked over to the bar where I'd set his urn and stared at it. The metal casing mocked me. I hated that he wanted me to do this. I hated that he was gone.

I hated that I didn't hate him like I wanted to.

I missed my dad. It killed me that I'd been such a disappointment to him. I should have been a better first-born son. I should have protected the family when he couldn't.

I should have protected Carson.

But they were all gone, and I was alone. The ability to ask for forgiveness—to make amends—was gone. The only thing I could do now was obey my father's wishes and hope that it made up for the fact that I'd been a shitty son.

I growled and grabbed the urn and headed back to the deck. I walked past Abigail who had her back to the railing and was watching me. I didn't stop until I was at the back of the boat, overlooking the churning water behind us.

I swallowed, emotions that I didn't want to acknowledge flooded to the surface, causing tears to prick my eyes. I didn't want to cry. I'd done such a good job up until now stuffing everything down, but I couldn't anymore. There was no hiding the fact that I'd lost my dad and my family was basically gone.

I twisted the lid and set it on the ground behind me. I closed my eyes, mustering my strength, and then I tipped the urn over. I opened my eyes to see a steady stream of ash fall into the murky water below. It was like everything was moving in slow motion.

This was my father. He was officially gone.

"I'm so sorry," I whispered, my words choking on my emotions as they tumbled from my lips. "Please forgive me."

I closed my eyes once more, praying that the wind would pick up my words and whisk them to heaven. I hoped that when Dad heard them, he would see I was trying to be a good son. That I was trying to make up for the mistakes I'd made.

Abigail remained quiet, which I was grateful for. With the urn now empty, I turned it back over and then held it against my chest. I said one final, "I'm sorry," before I grabbed the lid of the urn and twisted it back into place.

I didn't feel better, but I did feel as if a weight had been lifted off of my shoulders. I'd done what Dad asked. He couldn't be disappointed with me, at least for that task.

I glanced up to see Abigail was standing a few feet off. Her arms were folded across her chest, and she was studying me with an expression that I couldn't quite read. I gave her a weak smile as I passed by her and made my way into the cabin.

I didn't hear her following me until she slammed open the door and stalked into the room. "When were you going to tell me about Harmony?" Her tone was short and staccato. Like she'd been storing up her frustration.

"What?" I asked as I set down the urn and turned to focus on her.

Her cheeks were flushed, and I knew she was angry, but the color just made her more beautiful.

"Harmony? When were you going to tell me that your

family's company is behind the destruction of the town that took you in. That...cared about you."

Those four words startled me. When I looked up at her, I could tell that they startled her too.

"I just found out about it when I got here. I didn't know my family was a part of the buyout of the town."

Her eyebrows went up as her eyes searched mine. She seemed somewhat satisfied with that answer, but that only lasted a split second. "So, what are you going to do about it?"

Exhaustion coated my bones. I hadn't even thought about what I was going to do when she walked out of my life for good. Did she really think I had the energy to try to fight for Harmony?

"I don't know, Abigail. What can I do? The deal is pretty much locked in." I scrubbed my face with my hands before pushing them through my hair.

When I glanced back over to her, her eyes were wide, and I could see the tears starting to form in her eyes.

Shit. This wasn't good.

"So that's it, huh? You're just going to turn your back on the town and walk away. Throw your hands up and give in?"

I studied her. Was this still about the town? "What choice do I have?"

She sputtered a few times. "You have a lot of choices. You can stand up for yourself. You can say that this isn't fair. You can finally let yourself have what you want." She took a step closer, heat burning between our bodies.

I felt myself lean into her. I wanted to give in. I wanted to let my desires for her loose. I wanted to show her how I could love her like no other man ever would. But I couldn't. I'd promised Emery that I would fulfill my end of the bargain and marry Emmeline. It was how I was going to make up for what I did so long ago.

"You just have to say yes." Her gaze felt as if it were burning a hole into me. It was so intense, so raw, that it made my entire body ache.

I studied her, searching her eyes. I wanted to say yes. I wanted to say yes to her, to Harmony, to the family that I'd discovered there. "I can't," I whispered.

Her face fell at my words. I wanted to take them back. I wanted to be the man she thought I was...but I couldn't be. Not when I'd caused such destruction and pain. My life wasn't my own anymore. It belonged to those whose futures had been irrevocably changed by my actions.

A tear slipped down Abigail's cheek. Before I could stop myself, I reached up and caught it with my fingertips. Electricity shot through my body from that slight touch. I stared down at my hand before slowly bringing my gaze up to meet hers.

"I'm sorry," I whispered.

She studied me, chewing her lip as if she were biting back the words she wanted to say. I feared and longed for her to release her thoughts.

"Then let me do something for you," she whispered as she took a step closer to me.

Warning bells sounded in my mind, but I pushed them away. For this moment, I was going to let her take control. "Okay."

She lifted her hand as she rested her other hand on my shoulder. Then she slowly brought her gaze up to meet mine. "Dance with me?"

Her words settled in my heart, making it pound so hard I feared she could hear it. I knew I should say no and walk away, but I didn't have the strength. This was the last night I was going to see her, and I was going to be selfish.

My hand found her waist and slipped around and pressed against her back until her body was centimeters from me. Then I engulfed her hand with mine, welcoming the warmth and life I felt when I touched her.

We just stood there for what felt like an eternity. We were two lost souls who found ourselves in each other. For a moment, this moment, we were going to live.

She stepped closer to me, and I responded by tightening my grip on her. Then I slowly started to move my feet, and she welcomed my lead. We swayed in silence for a moment before I started to hum Frank Sinatra's "You'll Always Be the One I Love"—just like I'd seen Dad do all of those years ago.

That seemed to invite Abigail in, and slowly she leaned forward until her cheek was resting on my chest. I tipped my head down until my cheek was on the top of her head. I could smell her shampoo and feel her warmth. It was like I was in heaven or in a dream, and I never wanted to wake up.

"I'm breaking up with Anders," she whispered.

I stopped swaying. "What?" I asked as I pulled back.

She didn't move to meet my gaze. Instead, she remained pressed against me.

"I don't love him, and I'm certain he doesn't love me. I'm tired of trying to make it work." She paused before slowly looking up at me. "Make sure you see that he gets some help."

I nodded. "Of course." She didn't have to ask me. I was going to help Anders no matter what. He was my friend. He'd been there for me when I needed someone the most.

She studied me before she leaned against my chest. "Promise me something else."

I wrapped my arm around her back, crushing her to me. "Anything."

"If you don't love Emmeline, don't go through with the marriage. Emery told me about the arrangement. I know you think that you are doing something good, but making yourself miserable for the rest of your life won't bring your brother or your dad back."

I closed my eyes, wishing I could promise her. The truth was, I didn't love Emmeline. I loved Abigail. She was my person. The soul I was meant to find. But that didn't matter now.

"Bash?"

I groaned at the sound of my name on her lips. I closed my eyes to avoid her gaze, which had now tipped up to meet mine. I could tell that she was watching me, but I didn't have the strength to confront her.

"I can't..." I squeezed my eyes shut, wishing things could be different.

The feeling of her hand on my cheek shocked me. Then suddenly, her lips brushed mine for a brief moment, freezing me to my spot. I slowly opened my eyes to see her staring up at me. Her eyes were brimming with tears, and her lips were tipped up into a sad smile.

Then she rose up onto her toes once more, and I leaned forward until our foreheads touched.

She closed her eyes and took in a deep breath, then whispered the saddest two words she would ever speak to me...

"If only."

19

ABIGAIL

SWEET TEA &
SOUTHERN GENTLEMAN

Anders made a concerted attempt at trying to convince me to stay the next morning, but I'd already made up my mind. It was futile to stay with him and pretend I wasn't in love with his best friend. I told him we weren't meant for each other. And when I admitted that I'd kissed Bash, he didn't seem too shocked.

He said he suspected there might be something going on between us, but he figured it was just sexual tension and that was it. I told him, for me, it was deeper feelings, but if he wanted to know how Bash felt, he needed to ask him.

He flopped back on his bed and grabbed his phone, effectively ending our conversation. I didn't wait around for him to say goodbye or see me out. Instead, I rolled my suitcase from his room and down the hall. I released the extendable handle just as I got to the top of the stairs and slipped my hand into the top handle. I descended the steps as quietly as I could.

If Bash was up, I didn't want him to know that I was leaving. Last night had been torture, riding alongside him back to shore and then in the limo back to his house. Thankfully, he didn't try to make small talk. I think he realized that I wasn't in the mood, so he had Nicholas play soft music in the background to break up the silence.

When I got back to my room, I booked a flight and then tossed and turned the rest of the night. My mind was full of Bash, our kiss, and how he made me feel. I knew I was falling in love with him, and it made my heart ache that he didn't feel the same.

Or at least, didn't feel strongly enough to break off his fake engagement with Emmeline to be with me.

As soon as I got to the bottom step, I gingerly set my suitcase down on its wheels and made my way to the front door. My ride share wasn't here yet, but I wasn't going to spend another moment in this house if there was a chance I was going to run into Bash.

Just as my fingers wrapped around the door handle, I heard a noise next to me.

"Leaving so early?"

Bash's smooth voice made me close my eyes for a millisecond before I took a deep breath and turned to face him. His hair was damp like he'd just gotten out of the shower. He was wearing a white t-shirt that accented his tan and his muscles, along with a pair of pajama pants that made my whole body respond.

He was so unfair. He couldn't have just let me leave. He had to see me off.

"Yeah, my ride's about to be here," I said, offering him a weak and disingenuous smile.

He studied me before shoving his hands into his front pockets. I could see that he had things he wanted to say to me, and I prayed he would keep those words inside. My heart was already breaking; I didn't need it to be shredded with worthless platitudes.

"Oh," he said, his voice so low and gravelly that it came out almost like a growl.

"You'll be fine without me here. You have Anders and Emmeline." I waved toward myself. "I'd just get in the way."

"Abigail, you—"

"Plus, my shop needs me. Dad's been running it for a few days, and I feel like I'm taking advantage. Sabrina is in the middle of therapy, and then there's little Samuel. I'm sure he's walking and talking now. Babies. They change so fast." I was rambling now, and with each step that Bash took toward me, I only spoke faster.

"I don't love her, you know."

His words made my entire body freeze. I stared at him, begging him to continue, but at the same time, fearing what he was going to say. "But you have to. You're marrying her."

His eyes turned dark as if the cloud of reality had finally

surfaced. He stared at me before he scrubbed his face and took a step back. He cursed as he pushed his hand through his hair.

"It's okay. I'll be fine. You'll forget me as soon as I leave."

His expression turned pained as he stared at me.

"I promise," I whispered.

Three solid knocks on the door had me yelping and jumping to the side. I turned around, relieved that in mere moments, I was going to be out of here and away from Bash.

I pulled open the door.

"Abigail?" A middle-aged man with a ball cap and a stained hoodie was standing there with keys in his hand and an annoyed look on his face.

I nodded, grabbing the handle of my suitcase and heading out onto the doorstep. "That's me," I said, forcing myself not to turn around.

"Great. I've been waiting for five minutes."

I ducked my head. "I'm so sorry."

He just grunted.

He didn't help me put my suitcase in the back; he just clicked the key fob to pop the trunk. I hurriedly loaded my luggage and then made my way to the back seat, where I pulled open the door.

A hand caught the door, causing me to turn to see Bash standing there, his expression hard. His jaw muscles clenched as he stared down at me. "Let Nicholas take you," he said as he slowly tipped his head toward the driver, who had the window down and was staring at him through the side mirror.

I shook my head. I needed to get away from Bash. Even if that meant getting into the car with a man who looked like he knew the location of a few dead bodies.

"I'll be fine."

Bash shook his head. "No."

"Girly, are you going, or what?" The driver glanced up at me.

"Open the trunk back up. She's staying here." Bash turned so his entire body towered over the driver's side door.

The driver parted his lips as he stared up at Bash.

"I'm fine," I said, reaching out to touch Bash's hand that was still on the door, but then I stopped myself.

I could see Bash's gaze land on my hand for a brief moment before he returned his focus to the driver. "I will pay you a thousand dollars if you tell her you won't take her to the airport."

"Bash!"

But he wasn't listening. And now, neither was the driver. He glanced at Bash then over to Bash's house before shrugging. "Umm, 'kay," he said before looking at me. "Looks like I'm booked for the day, girlie."

The sound of the trunk unlatching drew my attention, and before I could say anything, Bash was pulling my suitcase from the back. Bash told the driver to text his Venmo information and rattled off his phone number. I didn't even have time to step back before the man just pulled forward, the motion shutting the door as he drove off.

His taillights were all I could see before they disappeared down the driveway and out the gate.

"I'm going to kill the security guard on duty," Bash mumbled under his breath as he headed toward one of the many garage doors that lined the far end of the house.

"Excuse me," I said as I marched after him. I had a whole lot of words to say to him, but I was struggling to find a coherent way of saying any of them. "I had it under control." I finally caught up with Bash, but it was only because he'd paused in front of the far-left garage door and was punching in a code.

I reached forward to grab my suitcase, but he just pulled it away from me. "I would have been fine," I huffed, annoyed that he was trying to control me.

He gave me a sideways glance before snorting and continuing to punch in the number. "Sure you would've."

"I would have been fine," I repeated.

"And I would have seen you on the five o'clock news as a missing person."

I forced a laugh as the garage door began to open. "I can protect myself."

He ignored me as he ducked under the door. "If he didn't try to kill you, you still would have died from the bacteria cesspool that was his back seat." He walked over toward a car that I was certain cost more than my entire apartment building and pulled open the driver's door.

There was a click, and the trunk slowly swung open. I was a mixture of annoyed and furious as I watched him dump my suitcase into the trunk and then press a button so it began to close.

"You know I'm not yours to protect," I stammered out.

He had been walking back to the front of the car, but my words must have thrown him off because he suddenly stopped right next to me. He stared straight ahead for a moment before he dropped his gaze down to meet mine. "What?" he asked.

I knew I should tear my gaze away from him. That looking at him was only going to break my heart more, but he needed to hear me say this. "I'm not yours to protect. You protect Emmeline, and that's it."

His jaw twitched, but he didn't say anything.

"Please, just leave me alone." My voice was barely a whisper now.

He frowned as he studied me. "Just go with Nicholas, and I promise, you will never see me again. I just have to know..." His voice broke as he glanced toward the ground. "I just have to know that you are safe."

Tears brimmed in my eyes as I took him in. The fact that this was probably the last time I was going to see him, talk to him, or hear his voice rattle in my mind, made me sad. I didn't want this to end, but we had no future. It wasn't fair for me to stay.

"I'll do it on one condition."

His gaze met mine once more. "What condition?"

I wrapped my hands around the strap of my purse and took a deep breath. "Promise me you'll find a way to save Harmony Island. It's all I have left, and I don't want to see it disappear and become some holiday getaway for the rich."

He stared at me. I could see him chewing on my words. Then he nodded and stuck out his hand. "Deal."

I stared at it for a moment, fearing what touching him would do to me before I nodded and slipped my hand into his. He held it for a moment, staring at it as if he were trying to commit the feeling to memory just like I was, before he shook it twice and then pulled back.

"Deal," he said again before he turned and walked away. "Stay here. I'll get Nicholas."

I don't know why I thought that Bash would come back out, but he didn't. Instead, Nicholas emerged, looking as if he'd just been woken up. He was wearing a jogging suit and a pair of sneakers. That was the first time I'd seen him in anything other than a suit and tie.

He smiled and nodded toward the car. He held the back door open for me as I climbed in. Then he started the car and pulled out of the driveway. I kept my gaze peeled for Bash, but he didn't come back outside.

I settled into the back seat as Nicholas drove further and further away from Bash's house until I could no longer see it. I sighed as tears once again rose to the surface. This was all over.

I shouldn't care. I should have never fallen for a man I could never have. But I did, and I had. I loved Bash. And I hated that it didn't matter if he loved me—we couldn't be together.

Nicholas offered to walk me into the airport, but I declined. I hurried out of the car and around to the trunk, where I pulled out my suitcase and yanked on the extendable handle. Nicholas finally rounded the back, but I was ready to be away.

I tossed him a quick goodbye and headed into the airport.

Five hours later, I pushed open my apartment door to find Penny and Sabrina standing in the kitchen next to a pan of what smelled like fajitas. All the strength I'd mustered at Bash's house and through the plane ride vanished, and tears started streaming down my face.

They both turned to watch as I hurried to my bedroom, and when I heard a soft knock on the door, I called to them that I was fine, that I was going to take a shower, and I would talk to them later.

That seemed to appease them because they didn't try to enter or knock again.

Once I was in the shower, I collapsed on the tub floor, wrapped my arms around my knees, and cried. The warm water beat down on me and mixed with my tears.

I cried for Bash. I cried for his family. But most of all, I cried for my broken heart and the fact that, no matter how hard I tried, I was never going to forget Bash.

He'd become a part of me, and there was nothing I could do about it. I loved him. But he would never be mine. And nothing short of a miracle would change that.

It was best for me to try to forget him.

It was the only way I was going to survive.

SWEET TEA &
SOUTHERN GENTLEMAN

It was a lazy morning at the B&B. I helped Rose cook and serve breakfast. Then we split up the rooms and bathrooms, and by early afternoon, all the chores were done. I grabbed a book and a glass of iced tea and settled on the hammock on the far end of the porch with Carmel at my feet.

She was getting better at listening and didn't sprint off every chance she got. I'd worn her out with an early morning walk—in the opposite direction than the one I'd gone on when I stumbled on Jax. Carmel was currently twisted onto her back with her paws in the air and her upper lip flopped down, showing off her teeth and gums.

I giggled as I went back to the scene I was reading. It was Jackson Richards' newest novel, and it had me hanging on the edge of my seat. I was having to read it in bits, or I was going to have a heart attack from anxiety.

The breeze picked up around me, so I closed my eyes

and tipped my head back, taking a deep breath. I loved the smell of summer. The trees. The fresh-cut grass. It was the smell of childhood, and for a brief moment, I missed the life I'd run away from so many years ago.

For a brief moment, I could see myself back here, living the slow life that came with a small ocean town.

"Get up," Rose's voice bellowed, followed by the sound of the screen door slamming.

I whipped my eyes open and sat up, spilling the leftover tea across my leggings. "Rose," I complained as I set my book down and stood, wiping the remaining droplets of tea onto the porch. "What could possibly be wrong?"

"Your mother called. The doctors have said she can finish recovering at home, and she asked me to go get her."

My entire stomach dropped out of my body, through the porch, and landed six feet under the ground beneath me. "She what?"

Rose just shook her head and made her way back into the B&B. My ears were ringing. I followed after her, ignoring the fact that I was leaving my book, my drink, and my *dog* outside.

"Why is she coming back early?" I asked. I was standing behind Rose as she stood by the check-in desk.

Finally, she turned around with her purse strap up on her shoulder and a wild look in her eye. "You know your mother. I'm sure the doctors are just tired of having her there."

That, I could believe. "She's coming back. For good."

Rose nodded as she pulled her keys from her purse. "Keep an eye on the B&B. I'll be back with her in tow."

"And she's staying here, for good?" I repeated as I followed her once again through the screen door and out onto the porch.

"For good, Claire." She paused. "Get this place ship-shape." Carmel took that moment to weave her way through Rose's legs. "And get rid of any traces of her." Rose's words seemed harsh, but her affectionate pat to Carmel's head told another story.

"I will," I said as I reached down and wrapped my fingers around Carmel's collar.

I held onto it and watched as Rose pulled out of her parking spot and headed down the road. I waited until I could no longer see her taillights before I slipped on my flip-flops and guided Carmel down the steps.

"Come on, Mom won't go back here. You need to be out of sight while I figure out a way to tell her that I want to keep you," I said as I walked her across the yard and over to the shed.

She was reluctant to go in, but once I started scooping food into her dish, she was right by my side, happily munching at her dinner. I made sure her water was filled, and just as I started to shut the door, a voice from behind startled me.

"Excuse me, ma'am?"

I let out a yelp, slammed the door, and turned to see an older woman standing there. She had white hair that was pulled back into a bun at the nape of her neck and what looked like a satin blouse with some sort of white substance dried on her shoulder.

"Yes?" I asked as I shielded the door with my body, praying that she hadn't seen Carmel.

"I'm so sorry to bother you. I would have asked Rose, but I think she just left."

"No, no problem at all." I started to walk away from the shed. "I can help you."

She sighed. "Great. I need to have some things dry-cleaned. I've been visiting my grandson, and he spits up."

"Of course," I said as I led her up the back porch steps and opened the door into the kitchen. "I can get you some names of places in town."

She paused and glanced over at me. "Oh. Rose said that you had a service?"

"Oh, yes. You're right." I walked over to the small cupboard next to the kitchen door. "Go ahead and gather your items and hang them here. I think I remember Rose saying that one of the cleaners comes by if there's something to pick up."

Relief flooded her face. "Wonderful." She paused. "My daughter is struggling, so I want to be there as much as I can."

I nodded. "I understand completely. We're here to make your stay as enjoyable and worry-free as possible."

There was a sparkle in her eye. "I do love these small

towns. You know, my daughter runs an inn up in Rhode Island."

I raised my eyebrows. "Really?"

She nodded as a melancholy expression passed over her face. "I miss her."

"What's it called? I'll have to visit there if I ever go up."

"The Magnolia Inn. My daughter, Maggie, runs it."

"The Magnolia Inn," I repeated under my breath. "I'll keep a note of it up here." I tapped my forehead.

She smiled and then startled like she remembered she was supposed to do something. "I'll get the clothes and bring them down here." Then she paused. "Thank you so much. My name is Penny, in case you were wondering."

"Claire." I gave her a smile. "And of course. I hope your stay here is wonderful."

As soon as she left, I flew into motion. There were dishes in the kitchen to be put away and the floor needed to be swept. I had half the floor done when there was a panicked knock on the back door. My heart pounded as I swept up the dirt I'd gathered into the dustpan and dumped it into the trash on my way to the door.

Was it Rose? Why was she back here? Something must have gone terribly wrong if she was coming in the back way while Mom was coming in the front.

"What?" I asked as I yanked open the door, expecting to see the frantic face of Rose.

Instead, it was Jax. And he was worried.

"Jax?" I asked as I leaned forward to see if there was anyone with him.

"Have you seen Samson?"

"What?"

He rose up onto his toes and peered into the kitchen. "My sister's dog, Samson. Have you seen him?" He finished scanning the kitchen and settled back down onto his feet, staring at me.

"No, I haven't seen *Samson*. What are you talking about? And why are you here?"

He left me and started walking down the porch to peer into the windows.

"He's not in there," I said as I moved to stand next to him, folding my arms and glaring at him.

"I was at the lake fishing, and he suddenly took off." He turned to stare out at the yard behind the B&B.

"Well, that was stupid."

He glanced over at me before he walked to the steps and jogged down them. "You're sure you haven't seen him? He took off in this direction."

I'd been busy cleaning. I hadn't seen anyone since...

"Crap," I whispered under my breath. When Penny had startled me back at the shed, I'd forgotten to put the weight in front of the door.

"What?" Jax asked.

I ignored him. I hurried to the shed and groaned when I saw that the door was ajar. I yanked it open to find Samson mounting Carmel.

"Jax!" I screamed.

That startled the dogs, and Carmel took off to one side of the shed while Samson stayed standing where they had been.

"Shit," Jax said from behind me.

"Your dog..." I started sucking in my breath as the realization of what had happened settled inside of me. "Your dog..." I said again, not being able to form words. I stuck my finger out at Samson. "Your dog...*babies*."

Jax was staring at me now. I knew I sounded like a crazy person, but I had just about had it. I was stressed. Mom was moments away from getting home. And Jax's dumb dog may have just impregnated my dog.

"Relax," Jax said.

I hated how his smooth voice could calm my grating nerves with just one word. But that was short-lived when the image of his dog on top of mine rushed through my mind. "Relax?" I asked as I reached out and poked his shoulder. "Relax? Your dog came in here and..." There was no way I was going to say the words that were floating around in my mind, so I just bit down on my lip and glared at him.

"Mounted your dog?" he asked.

I glowered at him. "Why didn't you have him fixed?"

He stared at me. "First, he's not my dog. He's my sister's. And second, why didn't you have *her* fixed?"

"Oooh..." I began to pace just outside of the shed. "Just like a man. Always blaming the woman."

He frowned. "What does that mean?"

I didn't know. My mind was racing a mile a minute. From the corner of my eye, I saw Samson stalking toward Carmel. "No!" I yelled out. I shooed him away from her, and Jax came in and grabbed his collar.

"Can you just get him out of here?"

Jax beckoned Samson to follow him, and he reluctantly left the shed. I glowered at Carmel, not for what had happened, but for the fact that my life just got infinitely more complicated.

When I shut the door to the shed, I made sure to place the weight in front of it. Jax was standing a few feet off. He looked apologetic, and I hated that. It was harder to loathe him when he looked like he truly felt bad.

"You know I'm going to help, right?"

I rested my hands on my hips. "What?"

He nodded toward the shed. "I'll do the right thing. I'll help take care of her."

I shook my head and then squeezed the bridge of my nose between my fingers. "That's very gallant of you, but it probably didn't do anything." I raised my gaze up to the sky. "Let's pray that it didn't do anything."

Jax didn't move, so I glanced over at him. He looked like he wanted to say more but didn't know if he should. I wasn't ready to talk to him, not with Mom's impending arrival.

"Please, just go. I'm sure she'll be fine. Just keep him away from here."

Jax's fingers tightened around Samson's collar as he nodded. "Of course." He started walking toward the tree line. I hated that he looked like I'd somehow wounded him. He had to know it wasn't personal. My mother would end up right back in the hospital if she knew that Jax had been here, on her property...with a dog.

"Jax," I called after him, not really knowing what to say, but knowing that I couldn't let him think I hated him.

He waved his hand at me but didn't turn around.

I didn't have time to chase after him, so I watched him disappear into the brush and vowed that I would find him later and explain. Right now, I was mere moments away from Rose pulling up that driveway.

I wiped my hands on my apron and hurried across the yard and into the kitchen. I washed my hands, shuddering at the image I'd stumbled upon in the shed, before I picked up the broom and started sweeping.

My vacation was over. Any sense of nostalgia I'd felt these last few days was about to dry up like a puddle in the desert.

Mom was on her way back to rule and reign, which meant I was back to being one of her subjects.

All hail the queen.

My father's house was too quiet.

The echo of the large grandfather clock in the living room rattled around the walls and wiggled into my brain, making my entire body twitch.

I was grateful that Abigail allowed Nicholas to drive her to the airport. I knew with him she would be safe. But that didn't mean I was content. I hated that she'd left. That I was never going to see her again.

Instead, I was stuck here engaged to a woman I didn't love, living a life I didn't want to live.

I cursed under my breath and stretched out my legs. I was sitting on the couch, trying to figure out what I was going to do. My heart was begging me to run after Abigail, but my head knew that wasn't fair to her. She could never be mine.

If I loved her, I would let her go so she could find some other man to make her happy.

I tipped my head back against the couch and took a deep breath. I closed my eyes and covered my face with my hands.

My life was a dumpster fire.

The sound of footsteps on the stairs had me glancing over to see Anders emerge from behind the wall. He was looking at something on his phone. He stopped when he got to the bottom of the stairs, chuckled, and then looked around, his gaze settling on me.

He frowned as he looked around the room. "What are you doing in here?"

"When are you going to go to rehab?" The words were out before I could think about the ramifications. I was angry at the world, but mostly me, and I was taking it out on my friend.

He raised his eyebrows. "I drink just like anyone else does," he said as he shoved his phone into his back pocket.

I scoffed. "No, you don't." I tipped my face back toward the ceiling. "Trust me, any excuse you're going to give me, I've said the same thing."

When he didn't answer me right away, I peeked over at him. He was staring at one of the bookshelves. A spark of hope ignited in my chest. Perhaps my words would encourage him to change.

"I'm hungry," he said as he turned and made his way to the kitchen.

And just like a damp blanket on a baby fire, my hope was extinguished.

Not wanting to let this go, I stood and followed after him. I needed a project to get my mind off Abigail, "I know it seems like you're untouchable, but you're not. Eventually, consequences will catch up with you."

Anders was standing in front of the fridge now. The door was open, and he was staring inside of it. He glanced over at me as he reached in and grabbed out the bottle of orange juice. Then he set it on the counter and started rummaging for a cup. I walked over and pulled open the correct cupboard.

"So, you kissed Abigail?"

His words made my entire body freeze. I glanced over at him as guilt washed over me. "I'm so sorry, man."

He unscrewed the lid of the juice and poured the bright orange liquid into the glass. "Why didn't you tell me?"

"Tell you what?"

"That you liked her. I would have stepped back." He took a long drink. "Abigail was fun, but I didn't see a future with her."

I narrowed my eyes, unable to squelch the rage that was rising up in my stomach.

He chuckled as he raised his hands. "I definitely didn't feel the way you so obviously do."

I pushed my hand through my hair and took in a deep breath. "I'm sorry," I whispered. "I shouldn't have done that. I just...panicked."

Suddenly the feeling of a hand landing on my shoulder reverberated through my body. I glanced up to see him standing next to me.

"I didn't know a lot about your life. You've always been so private. Next time, maybe trust me enough to tell me?"

I stared at him. He was the closest I had to a friend. I lost my family. I lost my life. But the one person who'd stayed by me was Anders. "Do you trust me when I say you need help?"

His gaze faltered for a moment but then he nodded as he pulled his hand away. "If you ask me to go, I'll go."

I straightened and turned to face him. "I want you to go. I'll pay for it. It'll be the best facility there is." I stuck out my hand. "Promise?"

He glanced down, and I could see he was chewing on my words. But then he slowly raised his hand, and we shook. "I promise."

For the first time in a long time, a smile spread across my lips. He returned the smile, and we shook a few more times and patted each other's backs. When he pulled back, he moved to lean against the counter behind him.

"So, when's the wedding?"

I frowned. "I think next month?"

He scoffed. "No. With Abigail."

I glanced over at him, hating that her name got my heart racing. "Oh. There's no wedding."

He quirked an eyebrow. "Oh, really? Why not?"

Was he serious? "Because I'm engaged to Emmeline."

I didn't like the way he was studying me. Like he had a secret he was a little too excited to share. He shifted his weight and pulled out his phone. "Does she know that?" He swiped his phone on and then turned it so I could see the screen.

I stared at it. At first, I didn't understand what I was looking at. And then the image of Emmeline locking lips with a familiar-looking man came into focus.

"What?" I asked as I took the phone from his hand. This had to be an old picture. I glanced at the date. It was from last night. That's why she didn't come with me on the boat? It was because she wanted to meet a guy? He looked a lot like the gentleman who had been on her computer screen the night we first met.

"Looks like both of you are with the wrong person," Anders said as he finished off his orange juice and set the glass in the sink.

The sound of the doorbell filled the air. Anders and I both turned toward the front door. Confused, I headed toward it only to see a figure standing in front of one of the sidelights.

"Emmeline?" I asked as her familiar red hair came into view. I pulled open the door. "What are you doing here?"

Her gaze dropped to the phone in my hand and regret flashed across her face. "You've seen," she whispered.

"I'll be in my room," Anders said as he hurried up the

stairs with a bowl of cereal. I didn't have time to respond. He was gone before I could form a coherent thought.

"Can I come in?" Emmeline asked.

I glanced over at her and then nodded. "Sure." I stepped out of the way, and she walked into the foyer, looking uncomfortable. I offered her a smile, wanting her to know that I wasn't mad.

"I'm really sorry," she whispered. "I shouldn't have done that."

I scoffed and shook my head. "Truth is, I kissed Abigail yesterday."

Her eyes went wide. "You did? When?"

"Before the memorial service."

"Oh." She glanced off into the distance for a moment before she turned her attention back to me. "I thought she was with Anders."

I scrubbed my face with my hands. "Yeah. I'm a jerk."

"Maybe we're all just trying to please the wrong people."

I dropped my hands and shrugged. "Yeah, probably."

Except, for me, it didn't matter. If I didn't fulfill my father's agreement, I would break Emery's heart. I'd already been responsible for her pain in the past, I wasn't going to do it again.

Emmeline leaned against the stair railing and studied me. "So, what are we going to do?"

I pinched the bridge of my nose. My head ached and I wanted my heart to stop feeling as if it were shattering into a million pieces. "We have to go through with the wedding," I whispered.

Emmeline didn't respond right away. I glanced up at her to see a storm brewing in her gaze.

"I'll make you deal," I said. "We'll be married on paper only. You can be with the guy in the picture." I waved toward Anders' phone, which I'd set down on the entryway table next to me. "I won't say anything. We can live different lives. Live in different places. I just...have to marry you."

Her eyebrows went up.

"I have to do this for Emery."

"Even if it means you're unhappy?"

I swallowed. My throat felt as if it were closing up. "Yes."

Emmeline stared at me. "Why?"

"Because she wants me to."

She studied me. "And you're fine with just giving everyone else a happy ending, but not yourself?"

I shook my head. "I lost my right to a happily ever after a long time ago. It doesn't matter now."

Silence fell around us. I could tell that Emmeline was trying to figure me out. She was waiting for me to tell her that I'd lied. That I wanted to call the entire thing off and run to Abigail. She wasn't wrong for thinking I wanted to do that. But she was wrong in thinking I would do that.

I made a commitment to Emery, and I was determined to keep it.

"There's nothing else you want?"

I shoved my hands into my front pockets as I glanced around the room and then settled my gaze on her. "Actually, there's one thing I want to discuss with you."

"Okay," she said slowly.

"It has to do with Harmony Island."

22

ABIGAIL

SWEET TEA &
SOUTHERN GENTLEMAN

Three Weeks Later

The doorbell rang so I hurried to open it. Shelby grinned back at me as she held up a bottle of wine in one hand and a bag of chocolate in another. "I'm ready to get my romcom marathon on," she sang out as I stepped to the side and let her come in.

Sabrina was out with Dad and Penny, taking Samuel to the ocean, so I'd asked Shelby if she wanted to come over for some girl bonding time. She'd happily agreed and offered to bring the treats.

I was desperately trying to remain happy, even though my heart felt dead inside, so I welcomed the distraction of having Shelby around.

"Wonderful," I said as I shut the door and followed her into the living room.

"I was thinking, *You've Got Mail*, or *Sleepless in Seattle*."

"So, Meg Ryan or Meg Ryan?"

Shelby feigned a shocked expression. "Meg Ryan is the queen of romcoms."

I chuckled as I grabbed a couch pillow, flopped down, and hugged the pillow to my chest. "I'm okay with either."

Shelby groaned. "You have to snap out of this, girl."

I closed my eyes and buried my face in the pillow. "I can't," I said, my words muffled.

The couch shifted beside me as Shelby sat down. "I think you need closure."

I peeked over at her. She was studying me. I could tell she was being genuine, so I straightened and met her gaze more fully. "How do I get that?"

She tapped her chin. "I think you need to call him. Tell him that you are over him and that you are moving on."

I chewed my lip. "Just, tell him?" I shook my head. "What if he answers?"

"Let's call his office and tell the receptionist that you want to leave a message." She grabbed her phone. "I think just speaking the words will help." She started searching on her phone for his company's contact information. She had the number pressed and her phone to her ear before I could respond.

"Mr. Torres' office," the nasally voice from the other end said.

"I'd like to leave a message for Mr. Sebastian Torres," Shelby said.

I shook my head and tried to pull the phone away, but she just leaned back, out of reach.

"Mr. Torres is out for lunch. I can direct you to his voicemail."

Shelby nodded at me. "That would be wonderful."

"May I ask who is calling?"

Shelby looked at me with a panicked expression. "His cake maker," she blurted out.

The woman on the other end paused before she said, "I'll connect you."

The sound of ringing filled the air. Shelby tossed the phone at me. I watched it land on my lap, but I couldn't seem to bring myself to pick it up.

Suddenly, the smooth sound of Bash's voice echoed from the speaker and made my entire heart squeeze. I missed the sound of his voice. I lifted the phone to my ear and listened with my eyes closed.

"...leave a message and I'll return it as soon as possible."

Beep

The silence felt deafening as I sat there. I wanted Shelby to call again, just so I could listen to that recording one more time.

"Speak," Shelby whispered next to me.

I nodded. "Hey, Bash. It's Abigail. I'm just calling to tell you..." I cleared my throat. What was I calling to tell him? That I loved him? That I would never be the same without him? That it wasn't fair that he let me love him and then walk away? "...that I'm fine," I managed out.

"I'm really fine, in fact. The shop is doing well. The town is doing well. Everyone is doing well." *Stop saying well.*

I refocused my brain. "I just hope that, eventually, you can find happiness as well. I hope your marriage to Emmeline works out. And that your relationship grows and blossoms into something special."

I paused, tears filling my eyes. I didn't want any of that, but I was focusing on closure here. If there were words I needed him to hear, this was my time to say them.

"I love you."

I heard Shelby suck in her breath. I glanced over to see her staring at me, her tears brimming just like mine.

"I will always love you. And I'm sad that we will never have a future. I'm sorry if this is hard for you to hear, I just... need to say these words or I will explode."

Shelby nodded and wrapped her arm around my shoulders.

"So, please forgive me for laying this at your feet. For making my feelings your burden. But I needed to say them."

I closed my eyes, tears slipping down my cheeks. I knew the next word I needed to say, but I wasn't quite ready. I took a deep breath and held it as I counted down from three. Then I blew it out and gathered my courage.

"Goodbye."

I pulled the phone from my cheek and pressed the end

call button. Then I tossed it into Shelby's lap and buried my face in my hands as the sobs started. Shelby kept her arm around my shoulders and just let me cry.

Soon, my tears dried up and I straightened. Shelby dropped her arm and reached forward, grabbing her bag of chocolate and ripping it open. She tipped the bag toward me, and I grabbed a handful.

"Put the movie on," I said as I waved toward the TV.

She nodded.

"I need to forget," I whispered.

One Week Later

"ARE YOU READY?" Penny asked after a quick knock on my open bedroom door. She was wearing a white button-down shirt and a pair of tan linen pants. That woman always looked like she belonged on the cover of a magazine even when she was casually dressed.

I nodded and finished pulling my hair up into a messy bun then grabbed my purse that I'd set out on my bed. I pulled the strap up onto my shoulder as I made my way toward Penny, who smiled at me.

"You look beautiful," she said as I passed by her.

I loved how willing and open her heart was to us. Ever since she came into Dad's life, our family felt a little more complete. They'd left a few weeks ago to return to Magnolia, but they'd vowed to come back often, and I loved that they were true to their word.

"You're so sweet," I said as I leaned forward and gave her a squeeze.

Dad and Sabrina were sitting on the couch watching a baseball game while Samuel snoozed in his bassinet next to them. Sabrina had changed so much in the last month that it hurt my heart. She was finally coming out from under the dark cloud she'd been under, and I was starting to see sparks of her old self come back.

"Get all the drama," she called out to us as we passed by them.

"You know there will be a lot," I replied.

"A lot of drama?" Penny asked as she followed after me.

"In the town of Harmony, there's drama around every corner," I said as I held open the door for her.

Betty Lou had called an emergency town meeting. We'd been meeting every two weeks, but today she'd called everyone in town and begged them to come to the community center. "Something big is going to be announced," she'd said.

I really wasn't interested in being there, but someone had talked to Penny about it, and she was interested in going. I offered to take her, even though, with the way I was feeling, I didn't care.

My call to Bash had made me feel better for about two thousandths of a second. After the adrenaline wore off, I just felt like crap. The poor man had already gone through so much. He didn't deserve me dumping all of my feelings on his voicemail.

He never called back, surprise, surprise. And just last week, I caught a photo of him standing with Emmeline at some fancy New York cocktail party. I almost broke down in the gas station when I saw it, but I held it together until I got to my car and then bawled behind my store until I was certain I was dehydrated.

Now, I did everything I could to keep him from my mind and to keep my heart in a lockbox away from anyone who could hurt me.

Penny kept the conversation light as I drove through town. The parking lot was full, so I had to find a place in front of a shop a bit further down the road. Once we were out on the sidewalk, Penny kept quiet, and we walked side by side toward the community center.

Betty Lou was talking when I pulled open the heavy metal doors. I sheepishly gave everyone a soft smile as Penny and I quietly entered the gym. There were only a few seats open in the back, so we snuck over and slipped onto the cold metal chairs.

"...this is incredible news for our small town. To be able to *partner* with Deveraux construction instead of handing over our buildings means a better town for us and more willing participants for them."

I frowned. "What are they talking about?" I asked Krystal, who I'd seen a few times working at the Honey Bee Library.

She glanced over at me and then back to Betty Lou. "I guess they no longer want to just buy us out. They want to give us grants to help fix up our businesses to encourage tourism."

"Ah," I said as I turned my attention back to the front. And then my entire body froze.

Betty Lou was introducing...Bash.

He was standing next to her in a black t-shirt and jeans. He looked so good that I wanted to cry and throw up at the same time. My hand found Penny's, and I squeezed it so hard she yelped.

"He's here," I whispered as I ducked down behind the people who were sitting in front of me. I narrowly missed hitting my head on the chair back.

"Abigail," Penny hissed as she leaned forward and tried to twist her hand free.

Realizing that I was probably crushing her fingers, I let go and covered my face in embarrassment. "I need you to help get me out of here."

Thankfully, she didn't ask any questions. She nodded and slipped off her chair, keeping her body hunched over in a futile attempt to hide me.

But I didn't care. Even if he saw me, I'd be gone before he could do anything. I'd hide out in the most obscure place in town until he finally left this place. Then, I would move far, far away where he could never just sneak up on me.

That was my plan, and it was brilliant.

Just as I neared the door, I heard my name. It was soft

and sent shivers down my spine. He was close. I could feel him. I wanted to look so bad, but I was scared of what that might do to me, so I just kept my hands on the door latch and took a deep breath.

"Abigail," he said again.

I closed my eyes, shook my head, pushed on the handle, and hurried out to the foyer of the community center. Thankfully, it was empty. The last thing I needed was for the town's busybodies to see me have a breakdown.

"Please, wait."

The feeling of his hand on my elbow stopped me. Electricity rushed through my body as I slowly dropped my gaze.

"What do you want from me?" I whispered, unable to look him in the eye.

"I...um..." His voice was soft and gentle, and I hated that.

Yell at me. Chastise me for calling you, but don't do this. Don't act like you care. Because then, my feelings would grow, and in the end, I'd be left alone with a deeper wound that would never heal.

"I'm sorry I didn't call you back."

I frowned and peeked up at him. "What?" That was a mistake. He was staring down at me, his gaze open and honest, and my heart swelled with the love that I'd been trying to convince myself I didn't feel.

"I didn't know you left me...a message."

Tears stung my eyes. "It's okay. I just left it so I could—"

"Get closure?" He nodded. "That's what I was told."

I chewed on my lower lip as I stared at him. "Is that why you came all the way down here?"

He glanced around. "Not exactly. I came down to talk to the town. But I hoped I would get to see you."

I stretched out my arms. "Well, you saw me." I dropped them back to my sides. "I should go." I stepped around him, ready to take off once more.

"Wait." His hand was back on my arm. "Please."

Why did he keep doing this? Didn't he know that he was killing me? "What, Bash?"

His hand lingered on my arm. His fingertips burned my skin. "I'm not marrying Emmeline."

I blinked once. Twice. Three times. "What?" I asked, when his words finally registered. Had I heard him right?

"Emmeline. I'm not marrying her anymore."

Emotions choked my throat. "What? Why?" I turned to face him, my gaze meeting his. If this was a joke, he wasn't being funny. But he looked genuine as he stared at me.

"I don't love her."

"I thought that didn't matter."

He winced. "It didn't at first. That was, until my sister-in-law, Emery, heard your voicemail. You left it while she was in my office. It made her angry enough to delete it. Then, I guess, Emmeline confessed to her that she didn't want to marry me and said we shouldn't be forced to marry if we don't want to."

"But your father..."

He shook his head. "He gave her the ability to call it off

if she wanted to. But Emery has been so mad at me for so long, that she wanted to see me hurt." He swallowed, his jaw muscles twitching. "I deserved that."

"No. You didn't."

He dropped his gaze. "When she realized that she was keeping me from the woman I loved and that hurting me would never bring back Carson, she released me from the obligation.

"Emmeline and I worked on an agreement together to present to the town." His hand slid down from my elbow until his fingers gently grasped mine. "But I'll admit, I may have had ulterior motives coming here." He dipped his gaze down to catch mine once more. "I mostly just wanted to see you."

He took a step forward. "I wanted to tell you that I love you. I will be yours if you still want me." He brought his hand up to my chin gently, so I had no choice but to look at him. "I love you, Abigail. I loved you the moment I met you behind your store. I tried to stop loving you. I tried to stay away from you. But I can't anymore. I want to be your husband, and I want you to be my wife." His gaze deepened. "Tell me you don't love me anymore, and I'll walk away for good."

My fingers slipped from his as I reached both hands to his shoulders and stepped forward. I wrapped my arms around him until my body was pressed to his. I rose up onto my tiptoes. "Never," I whispered in his ear.

His arms circled my waist as he lifted me from the

ground. He carried me through a closed door in the hallway and into a dark and empty room. But I didn't care. I needed him. I wanted him.

My lips crashed into his as he pressed me against the wall, caging me in with both hands. Our lips moved in sync as my hands roamed his chest, shoulders, and back muscles.

He freed one of his hands from the wall and threaded his fingers through my hair, angling my face so he could deepen the kiss.

My hands slipped under his shirt, and I could feel the planes of his stomach and chest. He growled and reached down, effectively stopping my roving hands.

"Are you trying to drive me wild?" he asked as he pulled away from my lips and stared down at me with a fire in his gaze.

My lips felt swollen, but I didn't care. I loved this man, and he loved me. That was all that mattered.

I gave him a sheepish smile, cradled his cheeks with my hands, and met his gaze head-on. "I love you so much, Bash Torres."

He tipped his forehead to meet mine. Then he brushed his lips against my nose, my two cheeks, and then finally against my lips.

"I love you, too."

23

CLAIRE

SWEET TEA &
SOUTHERN GENTLEMAN

My foot bounced as I sat in a waiting room chair at Paws and Pals, the veterinary clinic in Powta. Carmel sat at my feet, staring at the other dogs in the room. I wasn't sure if she felt my nervous energy or if she was just tired, but my stomach was in knots.

After I'd found her together with Samson, I wrote off the whole situation as a fluke, and I did a great job keeping Mom distracted enough so I could keep Carmel in the shed without her being seen. I even offered to stay longer to help her get on her feet.

Part of it had to do with the fact that my roommate called. Our whole building was evacuated for fumigation, so there was no hurry for me to come back. But the other part was that I got to witness how hard it was for Mom to help Rose with the B&B. And the guilt of keeping Carmel hidden away ate at me enough to make me promise to stay longer to help out.

We fell into a rhythm, until a month later I started to notice Carmel's sides getting rounder and her normally hyper behavior getting replaced with naps and slower movements.

Now, I was moments away from finding out if she was pregnant. But I was pretty certain I knew the answer.

"Claire and Carmel?" A vet tech asked as soon as she opened the door that led to the back.

"Present," I said, a bit too loudly.

An elderly woman stopped talking to her chubby white cat, which was currently hissing at Carmel, to stare at me. And so did the man in the back with some sort of creature in a pet carrier.

I gave them a sheepish smile as I stood and called for Carmel to follow me. The vet tech led us through the door, down the hallway, and into one of the small examination rooms.

I sat in one of the far armchairs while Carmel took her time walking around the room, sniffing every inch. The vet tech sat on the rolling chair and scooted it up to the computer.

"So, what brings Ms. Carmel in today?" she asked as she shook the mouse, and the screen came to life.

"Well, I think she might be pregnant," I said, the last word coming out as a whisper.

The vet tech glanced over at me. "What makes you

think that?" she asked as she returned her gaze to the computer and typed in a password.

I sighed. "She's getting fatter and more tired."

Another sideways glance at me. "It could be her food. How much have you been feeding her?"

"The normal amount." I took offense that she seemed to think I didn't know how to take care of a dog.

"Okay." She turned to face me as she rested her elbow on the desk. "To be pregnant, she needs to have been with a male. Has she been with a male?"

Was this person serious? "I understand how puppies are made," I said.

Her eyebrows went up like she didn't believe me.

"And yes, I witnessed her with my ex's dog a month ago."

"Your ex's dog?"

That's what she focused on?

"Why was she with your ex's dog?"

I sputtered, trying to come up with a response. "It's not like I chose for them to get together. You know dogs. *Can* they be stopped?"

Her eyebrows were almost to her hairline with how much she kept raising them. My cheeks burned as I wanted to melt under her scrutiny.

"Did you do this so you would stay in your ex's life?"

My mouth dropped open. How was this *my* fault? "Of course not," I whispered.

She pursed her lips before turning to the computer and typing a few things.

I collapsed against the chair as I blew out my breath. Of all the things I thought they would say to me, this was far from anything I'd imagined. My mind was still reeling when the vet came in after the tech took Carmel's vitals and excused herself.

The vet was an older man and, I hoped, less judgmental than the tech. He took to Carmel, scratching her ears before feeling her belly. The judgy tech came in a few minutes later with an ultrasound machine.

I stayed by Carmel's head while he ran the ultrasound wand over her stomach and declared she was going to be a mom.

I stood there, staring at the multiple wiggling beans on the screen. I must have looked pale, because the vet leaned forward with a sympathetic look in his eyes.

"I take it this wasn't planned," he said.

"The dad is her ex's dog," the tech said under her breath as she leaned in.

I shot her an annoyed look. "Not planned at all."

The vet sighed as he returned the wand to the machine. "This is why we emphasize spaying and neutering your animals."

There was a slight clip to his tone, which only made my cheeks burn hotter. I knew the lecture he was about to give me. I'd said it to so many pet owners back home. I knew what they were thinking and how irresponsible they must have thought I was.

They didn't know the whole story, and I didn't really feel like telling them. It's not like they would listen anyway.

I sat through the importance of getting her fixed once the puppies were born. How to help her through this pregnancy. And what to do as her due date approaches.

My body felt numb as I just nodded, took the pamphlets they handed me, and then followed them to the waiting room. I paid and wrapped her leash around my hand as I led her outside.

Once she was safe in the car, I shut the door behind her and climbed into the driver's side. I slammed the door and then just sat there, staring at the flower planter in front of me. Realization hit me as I grabbed the steering wheel and rested my forehead on my knuckles.

I closed my eyes, fear clinging to my chest. Things with Mom had been tolerable. I did what I could to help her around the B&B, and our fighting had become an uncommon occurrence.

It must have been because I was hiding Carmel, but I just let her little snide comments about me slide without putting up a fight. That seemed to appease Mom, and it helped soothe my guilty conscience.

But now, with Carmel pregnant, things were about to change in a big, big way.

My hands shook as I reached for my purse and found

my phone. I found the number for Harmony Pub and pressed it. Three rings sounded before Jax picked up.

"Hello?"

I paused and closed my eyes, taking a moment to gather my thoughts. I heard him inhale like he was about to speak again, so I blurted out, "You're going to be a father."

24

JUNIPER

The sky was ominous as I pulled into the back lot of Godwin's Grocery and turned off the engine of my car. My hands were shaking, but they'd been shaking ever since I left Texas and drove straight to Harmony Island.

I blew out my breath and closed my eyes, wrapping my fingers around the steering wheel.

"You left. He's gone. He's not going to come after you," I whispered under my breath.

I let those words sink in, even though my entire body wanted to reject them. I opened my eyes and glanced into my rearview mirror, wincing at the black eye that stared back at me.

It'd gotten worse during the drive. I knew as soon as Mom saw it, she was going to lose her mind. But I couldn't have her react that way. I was barely holding it together. The last thing I needed was a mother hen circling around me and muttering under her breath that she'd known Kevin was wrong for me.

That I should have never married him and left town.

Kevin and I had that love fast, love hard kind of relationship. I should have known it wasn't going to last. But I'd believed in true love and that he was my knight in shining armor. No one could have convinced me otherwise.

If only I'd known then what I knew now.

I reached up and gingerly touched my puffy eye. I winced as a jolt of pain akin to lightning pulsed through my body. I hissed and lowered my hand. That had been a mistake.

Knowing I couldn't sit in my car for much longer, I pulled the door handle and climbed out. The first few drops of rain fell on me as I pulled out my suitcase and purse and hurried to the back door of the grocery store. I knocked two times before the door burst open. Dad was standing there with his neatly trimmed mustache and his readers perched on the tip of his nose.

"Juniper?" he asked, his gaze shifting to my eye and staying there.

"Hey, Dad," I said as I stepped past him, dipping my face in an effort to hide my bruise.

"Wha—"

"Rich, who is it—Juniper?" Mom rushed over to me and took my face in her hands. She tipped it from side to side, and I could see the fury burning in her gaze. "What happened?" Then her eyes narrowed as she stared at me. "Did he do this to you?" she asked.

I pulled back, not wanting to answer. I was exhausted, and my mind hurt from all the questions I'd asked myself as I drove. I didn't have the energy to try to process hers. "I'm fine, Mom," I said as I sidestepped her. "I'm just tired."

"Juniper," Mom said. I could feel her gaze on me as I made my way to the office to sit down.

"Betty," Dad said in a hushed tone. I made a mental note to thank him later.

"But, Rich, this isn't okay."

I was inside the office, but I could still hear her talking. I collapsed on the seat and tipped my head back, letting my hands drop to my sides.

"Now is not the time to drill her," Dad said.

Mom tsked, and I didn't have to see her to know that she had her arms folded across her chest as she chewed on her thumbnail. "I don't care that his family rules this town. It's not right what their son did to our daughter."

"I know."

"Proctor or not, he needs to pay."

***

I hope you loved Bash and Abigail's story. And don't fear, they will continue to be a big part of the series, so you'll see the progression of their romance.

Make sure to grab your copy of Godwin's Grocery from

me HERE. I can't wait to share Claire and Juniper's story with you.

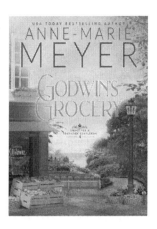

I also wrote a bonus scene from Shelby's POV. I have two different versions. A spice one, which is designed for 18+ readers and a sweet one that is closed door. I hope you enjoy them. You can get either scene for FREE when you join my newsletter. Here is the link:

Shelby and Miles **SPICY** Bonus Scene: HERE
or scan below:

Shelby and Miles ***SWEET*** Bonus Scene: HERE
or scan below

The bonus scene will be emailed via BookFunnel. They can
send it to your preferred e-reader. You can find help at
www.bookfunnel.com/help

If you haven't checked out my Red Stiletto Bookclub series,

you're missing out! Abigail, her dad, and Penny come into the stories. You'll love them. Grab your series bundle HERE or scan below.

For a full reading order of Anne-Marie's books, you can find them HERE.
Or scan below:

Printed in Great Britain
by Amazon

30119436R00148